SACRIFICED TO THE WARRIOR

VERONICA DEAN

PROLOGUE

THE GLOBAL GAZETTE

Arkgan, June 21st, 100

Reported by: Mya 1721

———

Earth Ambassador Selected

———

23 days after the announcement of a nation-wide lottery to determine the select for the highly sought-after position, the world has itself an ambassador. The select is one Avi 2564 of the 33rd District. The announcement, made yesterday, has invoked outrage globally, nowhere more

than here in Arkgan, home of the Planetary Government. Member of the PG Xandr 4521 called the selection 'a travesty.' He continued: 'The decision of the Supreme Leader to hold a lottery was one of great wisdom and fairness, however, it was an oversight to include underling districts in the selection process. We all know that the select is of the greatest importance to the future of our entire world and race. How can we trust this massive responsibility to a savage?' Xandr 4521 found support throughout the PG and city, however, the Supreme Leader, in a statement to the media, assured the public that steps were being taken to ensure that Avi 2564 would be the perfect representative for our planet. 'We must put our trust in the Nepharans. They have dealt with Zahoth for millennia, and their delegates have assured me that this is the most prudent way to proceed. As we speak, an envoy is headed for District 33 to collect the honored Avi 2564 and preparations for the arrival of the Zahothians will commence. The PG, our visitors from Nephara, and I ask the great people of earth for patience and understanding as we handle this delicate situation,' stated the Supreme Leader.

Although Xandr 4521 rescinded his statement shortly after delivering it, his words sparked civil unrest globally and led to multiple incidents requiring intervention by the Global Security Bureau. Fortunately, our brave patriots crushed the traitorous uprisings with ease and those involved, including Xandr 4521, have been reprimanded.

The visit from Zahoth comes on the eve of the expiration of the 100-year peace treaty between humans and the evil Zahothians. In an address to the people, our wise Leader had this to say: "The barbarous invasion of our home by the alien race led to the death of almost 5 billion people. Our brave soldiers fought gallantly, however, the Zahothians are a race of pure evil whose only objective is to conquer every planet they come across. Luckily, our forefathers have led us into a time of peace and prosperity. The global state is now thriving socially, economically and diplomatically. So, although this is a time to honor the countless sacrifices our ancestors gave, it is also a time for thanks. The war, although devastating, allowed our new world to rise from the ashes of the old - stronger and wiser than before. It is also a time to give thanks to our friends from the stars -- the Nepharans. Without their crucial aid in the darkest hour of the conflict, it is possible the evil Zahothians would have destroyed the entire planet and every living soul with it. Our new world is in the greatest of debts to them for the generous sharing of their knowledge and technology. As everybody knows, the Nepharans were crucial in the development of the Azidoazide bomb, which once and for all crippled the alien aggressors. This technological invention will shield earth from any future invasion. However, this is not a time for complacency. The 100 year peace treaty between our two planets is coming to an end. In accordance with the treaty, a human female must be provided to the Zahothian ambassador for the purpose of breeding. The importance of this stipulation in the treaty has been emphasized by our Nepharan brothers. They say it will be impossible to maintain peace without this. Therefore, the ultimate sacrifice must be asked of one of this planet's strong women to ensure peace for our race for centuries to come. The Planetary Government will do its utmost to ensure that the peace and prosperity our planet has enjoyed for the past 100 years will continue on into the glorious future, but ultimately the responsibility is yours." The address was given to a record-breaking crowd and ended to thunderous applause and cheers of approval.

As per the regulations of the peace treaty signed almost a century ago, a child of Zahothian and human origin must be borne as a sign of the everlasting peace between the two planets. The Zahothian Ambassador will be the first Zahothian to set foot on the soil of earth since the treaty was signed. Nepharan intelligence tells us that the ambassador was himself a part of the unprovoked onslaught on humanity and is said to be one of the planet's fiercest warriors. Our fearless Supreme Leader had this to say on the subject: "we do not care who this alien is. Humans have proved that we bow down to no one. He may have slain our kind a century ago, but he is in a for a rude awakening when he arrives on this planet. We are stronger, wiser and better-prepared than before to face this evil creature. The entire population of our mighty planet can rest assured that the ritual will be carried out as planned, guaranteeing the freedom of you, our people, for eternity."

The Ambassador will be the first Zahothian to be allowed on to the planet since our glorious victory a century ago. He is expected to arrive on planet within the next 3 days. His ship will be parked in a private, undisclosed location outside of Arkgan for the duration of his stay. The Supreme Leader assured our people that this monster will not stay on earth a second longer than is necessary for the ratification of the peace treaty. However, at this time he did not give a comment as to how long this may be.

Our thoughts go out to Avi 2564 who is about to make

the greatest sacrifice for our planet that we can possibly imagine. The Supreme Leader has assured us that she will not be harmed during the process. Little is known of Avi 2546 other than the fact that she is a young worker from a mining region in District 32. However, all of that is about to change as her Cinderella story is complete and she becomes known to every man, woman and child as the hero of our planet. She is truly a role-model for every underling. And we wish her the greatest of luck in her honorable endeavor.

May our fearless Leader guide us to eternal peace and prosperity!

Chapter One

AVI

WHY WOULD I strike a guard again?

This was the only question in my mind as I ran down the shining metal corridor. I did not know where I was heading. I knew there was no escape, but running seemed like the natural thing to do when you are being chased by a gang of black stormtroopers with tazing prods. This was not the first time I had gotten in trouble. In fact, it was my third serious offense, and I had never heard of someone with a fourth one. My first offense was for stealing some extra rations from the cafeteria. They were easy on me then since I was so young, only 10 lashes. Since then I had learned to steal much better and haven't been caught for that in ages. My second happened when the dick head guard, Bracken, squeezed my ass while I was in line waiting to go down for the day. I turned around and punched him straight in the nose; I didn't even know it was him, I would have punched anyone who grabbed me like that first thing in the morning. Of course, it had to be the head of security forces for the entire mine. There were almost 10,000 employees here, 1,000 of them were guards and he controlled all of them. Needless to say, he did not take kindly to my 'insolence,' as he so eloquently put it. That time, my punishment was more severe and, let's just say, it made me really eager not to come into contact with those prods again.

This time, an asshole guard, once again, took me by surprise. I was walking back to my quarters after a long day in the depths. I was not in the best of moods after spending the last 10 hours in the pitch-black cavern surrounded by sweaty humans and that awful sulphurous smell that emanated from the mines, and, therefore, was really not in the mood to talk to anyone. Next thing I know, a guard, who I have never even seen, walks straight up to me and pushes me to the wall. He must have been new here and thought he could do whatever he wanted with the underlings, but even though we were basically slaves down here, we were protected from sexual harassment and abuse by law since we were not deemed fit to procreate even amongst our own caste. Not to say that it did not happen frequently, though. The mine needed new workers, didn't it? It was one of those open secrets hat everyone knew about, but no one ever talked about. Before he could thrust his lips on my face, I landed a massive blow to his testicles with my knee. He fell to the ground immediately with a loud groan. I was quite pleased with myself until I saw the two guards on the other side of the hall looking straight at me.

So, here we were. Even though I knew these corridors like the back of my hand, having lived here for my entire life, I could not outrun -- I steal a quick glance back at my pursuers -- seven guards for too long. I decide my best bet is to just run through the main exit, hopefully the guards will be off their game and I can dash through security unharmed. The biggest problem was not getting through security, it was what to do after that. The mining facility was surrounded by at least 10 miles of wintry forest in every direction. I was wearing a thin jumpsuit and sandals. I would probably be dead within a day even if I did miraculously make it through security, but if I stayed here, I would most likely have to face euthanizing and having seen a few of these events myself, I was unenthusiastic to be a part of it. I turned the corner towards the cooking zone. Maybe I could lose a few of the guards in the steam. Suddenly, a giant thump on my chest and my back is crunched on the cold iron floor grates. I felt like every ounce of oxygen had been knocked out of my lungs; I gasped for breath in desperation on the floor. I look up and see Bracken holding a baton.

"Well, well, if it isn't Avi 2564. It's a pity to see such a pretty little girl go down such a bad path."

He looked down at me with a smug smile as I still attempted to suck in as much air as possible with little success. "Take her to the corrections unit," he ordered the guards sternly.

One of the faceless drones walked up to me, raised his club and brought it down on my right temple.

I awoke, still dazed, in complete darkness. Was I dead? No. As my eyes adjusted to the blackness, I could make out the walls of the cell. I was strapped to some kind of device. I could not move my arms or legs. My body was in an X position and I felt very cold. I was pretty sure I had no clothes on. Suddenly, a noise in the darkness behind me and with the flick of a switch, a single light hanging from the ceiling illuminated the room. As I suspected, I was completely naked and tied to a series of metal bars with leather straps. My heart began racing as I heard slow footsteps behind me as well as a rustling of metal objects. I was suddenly extremely self-conscious that someone was seeing my entire body and felt an uncontrollable blush of shame invade my face.

"You know , Avi, I didn't want things to end up this way. I took a shine to you from the very beginning. You aren't like the other underlings. You have a certain spunk in you, a fire burning inside you. Unfortunately, fire can be dangerous and that's why you're here, in this precarious position."

I immediately recognized Bracken's ridiculously deep voice. I always suspected he was putting it on to seem tougher than he actually was.

"Bite me, Dickhead," I said, attempting to mask my fear the best I could. There was no way I was going to give this guy the satisfaction of knowing he made me feel anything other than disgust.

Bracken let out a slight arrogant chuckle as he continued, "Oh, I will baby, don't you worry."

Before I could react with another insult, I felt a sharp sting on my back. The sensation was unmistakable; I had just been given, what I assumed to be, my first lash of many. When you see someone getting whipped you think that it must just hurt like hell on the part of you that is struck, but no, you feel it in your whole body, every lash is like a lightning bolt to the heart that leaves you completely stupefied in agony. I was fighting back the urge to scream out in pain as I felt the next one on my right shoulder. I gasped in shock as my long blond hair fell down over my face.

"Now that you've had a taste of what is to come, my dear, maybe we can have a reasonable conversation."

Bracken seemed to be waiting for a reply but I said nothing. "I will take your silence as a sign of agreement," he said in that excruciatingly annoying tone of his. It almost hurt more than the whip.

"I have a proposition for you. I am in need of a personal assistant. I don't want this assistant to be just anyone. I want it to be someone I'm... drawn to. Yes, I could choose any of you filthy underlings to serve me, but there would be no fun in that. I don't need you, but for some reason, I do want you."

There was no way I was going to agree to this preposterous proposal. I would rather die than be a servant to a man like this. Before I could tell him how much this idea detested me, he moved within a foot of my face, lifted my face with his bony finger, so he could see my eyes, and continued, "before you answer, consider your options. I am the only one who has the power to save you. If you do not agree to this you will, after a considerable amount of torture, be euthanized in front of everybody, most likely as soon as tomorrow morning. Your last hours on this earth will be ones of excruciating pain and humiliation. On the other hand, you can work for me. Who knows, in time, you may come to like or even love me. I am very good to those who show me loyalty, and as the direct subordinate of the captain of the security forces, you would have certain perks. You could move out of that shit box you call home and move up to the top floor away from your

wretched caste. You would not be one of us, of course, but you would be as close as you can get to our status. I advise you to think this over carefully, as this is a one-time offer."

I didn't even have to think about it. I spat straight in his face and said, "fuck off and die, turnkey scum."

He wiped his cheek of the saliva slowly oozing towards his weak chin and gave a rapid, somewhat phoney smile. He slowly walked back behind me, so I was unable to see him and with a scoff said, "you really are a feisty one. It's a shame that won't be the case for long." He picked up something from the table and returned to me, putting his face right in front of mine. I could smell his foul breath as he said, "I'm going to enjoy breaking you. I bet you remember this, don't you?" he asked, indicating to the tazing prod in his hand. I attempted to mask my fear as best I could, but my eyes let me down.

"Ah yes, do I detect a flicker of fear? I myself have never been stung with one of these, but I've heard it's excruciating. If you do it in the wrong spot, you can kill a man. Or a woman."

He pressed the button at the far end of the prod which created a surge of blue electricity between the fang-like objects at the end of the weapon. I winced since it was so close to my face that I could practically feel the heat. He smiled and circled me. I hated that I could not see him. Suddenly, I felt the cold metal on my upper back. I was shaking with fear as I felt the prod explore my body lower and lower. Time is going excruciatingly slowly at this point, the anticipation of the shock is almost worse than the shock itself. He continues to torture me by swiveling the device all over my back. Finally, he reached my ass and I could feel his disgusting gaze violating me as he paused the movement for a second. He then brought the prod back upwards towards my side and as it reached my ribs, I felt the shock finally run through my body. I convulsed against my restraints and screamed out in pain and horror.

"You ready to reconsider? That was just a quick one. This night is only the beginning. By morning I'll have you begging me to be my servant."

I was sucking the air in trying to regain my senses and took a deep breath and said, " I would rather die."

"That can be arranged," he answered severely and stung me again in the middle of my arched back. This one was longer, and I spasmed uncontrollably for what felt like a lifetime. Finally, he let off and allowed me to sloop down on my restraints and regain my strength.

"We'll come back to the electricity later. First, I want to mark you some more."

He pulled out the whip and without further ado began furiously slicing my back. The pain was extreme, but after the prod, I was able to endure it. With the last couple of lashes, I could feel that he drew blood. He stopped and picked up the prod once more and circled my naked, bleeding body, admiring his handy work. As he circled me, I could see his tiny dick was hard through his pants. The sick fuck was getting off on this.

"I've always wondered what it would be like to fuck an underling, you know. You're such filthy beings, but so like us physically. I can't help but get aroused by your naked form. I bet you would also like to know what a man's cock inside you feels like before you die, wouldn't you?" he asked with lust in his beady little eyes. A tear came to my eye as he circled my body once more, and I heard the zip of his pants open. I couldn't believe this was about to happen. I closed my eyes and mumbled prayers to anyone and anything to save me from this hell. He grabbed my ass with both hands as his pants fell to the floor. I prayed for death as his long finger nails jabbed into my supple flesh.

"I'm going to enjoy this," Bracken said, licking his lips in delight.

Suddenly, a loud thump at the door.

"Go away," he yelled in anger.

The banging continued and became louder.

"This better be fucking important," my torturer mumbled as he reluctantly pulled up his pants and walked to the door slowly. He flung it open with an air of arrogance and was surprised to see a very tall, dark man with a bushy mustache and a military uniform with hundreds of badges attached to it.

"What in the Leader's name is the meaning of this, Captain!" he roared in fury.

Bracken mumbled something about punishing a prisoner and third strike before the giant man grabbed him by the throat and pushed him against the wall. "General, please," Bracken begged as he struggled for air under the soldier's mighty hand.

"You dare to abuse your position in this manner, do you have any idea who this girl is? Do you not watch the news, you little insect?"

Bracken continued to struggle for air and attempted to explain to the general that the satellite antenna had malfunctioned and nobody knew how to fix it. It's true, I hadn't seen anything of the outside world for months.

"Unacceptable captain. Release Avi 2564 immediately and then report to HQ. I will be sure to let your direct superior know of everything I have seen here."

The general, finally, released Bracken from his grasp and he fell to the floor coughing up phlegm onto the steel floor.

"Pathetic. I will do it myself."

My savior walked over to me and unfastened the straps, I fell to the floor and two of the general's men walked over to me and covered me with a blanket.

"I'm sorry this happened to you, my dear. I assure you that the captain will be dealt with in the harshest possible manner." The general whispered to me in the kindest tone I had probably ever heard from a superior.

All I could utter was, "thank you, thank you."

"Yes, yes, the gratitude can wait. We are on a tight schedule, so forgive me for the following necessity." I looked up and saw the general signal one of his men forward, who then injected my neck with a needle and the room went black instantaneously.

Chapter Two

AVI

I WOKE up in the most comfortable bed I had ever felt. It was like laying on a soft breeze. I looked up and discovered the room was as luxurious as the bed. The floors were all a deep-colored mahogany and looked ancient. Right across from me there was a massive screen along with two black leather sofas. To my right there was a beautiful bay window with a view of buildings taller than the skyline and a million lights. The light filled the room even though it was pitch black outside. I noted that I was no longer naked and had been dressed in a simple gown, much like they had at the hospital ward back home. Where the hell was I? The last thing I could remember was the general cutting me loose, then everything went dark. My mind delved deeper into the memories, but the trauma of the events made me stop and shut them out. I hope they fucking kill that Bracken.

I did not have much time to muse due to the doors suddenly flinging open. The abruptness of the action startled me, and I grabbed my silky cover in shock. Two figures appeared in the doorway. One was a tall blue crea-ture with a long ponytail and a long face. He (I presume it was a he) was wearing a long elegant robe covered in various patterns and colors. I'm pretty sure he was from the planet Nephara. I had obviously learned about our history in basic training for the mine, and our books contained photos of these creatures, although I had never seen one in person before. They were much taller than I had expected also he looked quite flimsy and gawky. In the pictures they had always looked rather dignified and even somewhat attractive. The second figure needed no intro-duction, I rubbed my eyes in disbelief as the large plump man walked towards my bed followed by the alien. He looked a lot like his portraits in some ways; he stood very tall and straight and had a big bushy moustache, however, his complexion was much less unhealthy in person, his face was quite red and he seemed much older and wrinklier than in the paintings hung around the living quarters of the mine. However, he did still look quite dignified in his black military uniform I had become so accustomed to seeing him dressed in. I almost felt like I knew him, having seen countless addresses by him and being surrounded by his image for the entirety of my life. The supreme leader reached my bed and sat down right next to me as I still lay under the covers.

"How are you, my dear?" he asked with grandfatherly concern.

I was a little distracted by the massive alien behind him and stuttered a little but was finally able to blurt out an abrupt: "fine."

"Don't worry, we come in peace," the alien said with a chuckle, noticing my curious gaze.

His attempt at humor made me feel more at ease as the supreme leader continued, "you must be very confused as to what is happening. I have been told that you have had a communications breakdown for the last month or so and have no idea what has been happening in the world. I take it you have not even heard of the global lottery?"

I shook my head in response.

"I assure you that the leaders of your facility and district are being punished for their negligence as we speak, however, we have more pressing matters to attend to. Why don't you pick yourself out of bed and come sit over at the table with us and we will explain everything?"

The image of Bracken being tied up like I was some hours ago made me giddy. The supreme leader gracefully gestured towards the table set in the corner by the window, and they waited for me to get up and move towards it before following suit themselves. They walked and talked with such an air of dignity and decorum which I had never before experienced; but I could not help but wonder why these two exceedingly important men were taking this much time to talk to an underling of a mining facility. Although I felt relatively at ease in their presence, I had this terrible feeling in my gut that not everything was quite right. Nonetheless, we all sat down at the table overlooking what I now realized was Arkgan, the capital city of our entire planet. I never in a million years thought I would have the chance to visit this place.

"You must be hungry," stated the supreme leader, rather than asking. He picked up the phone on the table and asked for some breakfast to be brought up to his 'special guest.' Now, I was really wondering what the hell was going on. The supreme leader was ordering breakfast for me. This was insane.

"I will cut right to the chase here Avi 2564. Please do not interrupt while I explain the situation."

I nodded in agreement and the supreme leader, in turn gave me a smile and a nod, and then proceeded to explain: "as I am sure you are aware, despite the recent communications breakdown in your region, the 100-year anniversary of the great planetary war is coming up. And as you know, the peace treaty signed with the Zahothians will come to an end. In accordance with the treaty, a child must borne of Zahothian and human decent to ratify the treaty and continue the peace indefinitely."

At this point, the Nepharan placed his hand gently on the leader's shoulder and cut in, "this may sound odd to humans, but it is a very common practice among intergalactic cultures. The melding of the blood constitutes a bond that cannot be broken and, given time, the DNA of both species will carry on into a new epoch of peace."

The Nepharan released his light grip from the leader and almost robotically he continued his explanation, "exactly. The practice will create a new species and set a trend for inter-species mingling among the population. However, the first time can be a little tricky and success is not always guaranteed. Not all aliens can mate with one another due to differences in biology, however, in this case, our scientists believe it to be possible. Now, this is where you come in. For years we devised plans of how to select the female with the best chance of success, but ultimately, even with our advanced technology, we realized that it would be impossible to determine the outcome, therefore, we decided on a lottery of all women from ages 23 to 28, the age we have determined to be most fertile among our species. And, you, Avi 2564 were our lucky winner."

I stared at the supreme leader dumbfounded, trying to process all the information that had just come my way. In training we had heard that the Zahothians were the fiercest warriors in the entire universe and that they had massacred not millions but billions of humans in the war. They were said to be over 10 feet tall and come from a planet of absolute evil. They felt no emotions, had no empathy, no remorse, their only instinct was destruction. And they wanted me to have sex with one of these monsters!?

My disbelief quickly transformed into anger and, without thinking, I blurted out, "you've got to be fucking kidding me." The supreme leader's face turned more serious, and I quickly corrected, "I mean... I'm sorry, Sir, but knowing what I know about the Zahothians, I really do not think this is something I want to do. You are asking me to mate with a... a monster."

The supreme leader placed his hand over mine and his expression returned to that of a warm father; a distinct contrast to the glimpse of stern leader I had witnessed a second ago. "We understand this is a shock, but you must understand that you will be the savior of humanity, if this treaty is not consolidated it could mean another war."

"But why me?"

I cut him off before he could answer; I am an underling. All I have done is worked in a mine. Why am I being trusted with this duty?"'

Both the Nepharan and the supreme leader looked at

me with a mix of surprise and amusement. "Because you won the lottery my dear," the old man answered.

"I don't think you realize what an honor this is. Your name will go down in the history books. The fact that you are so unwilling to serve your country is starting to become a little suspect. Do you not love your planet Avi 2564?"

"Well, yes, of course, but..."

"There are no buts, underling, either you love your planet or you don't," the supreme leader said in a severe tone. The mood had become tense, and I suddenly felt like I was in an interrogation rather than a friendly chat.

I realized that it was useless to resist. For a second, I had thought that I might have a say in the matter, but it became clear to me that this was an order, not a request. What was a simple underling to do up against the supreme leader? Therefore, I reverted to my formal tone that I had perfected throughout my life talking to superiors at the mine, "yes, supreme leader, I love my planet."

"That's good to hear Avi 2564 because if you refuse this honor. We will have to return you into the hands of your security captain, Bracken, is it?" the supreme leader said in a menacing tone.

I flinched at the thought of going back to that place. Only torture and certain death awaited me there. Who knows, maybe these guys were telling the truth, maybe I would survive and become a hero. This could be my ticket out of the hell they call District 32.

"No, sir, that will not be necessary. I am happy to accept this great honor," I said in my most convincing and patriotic voice.

In response to my agreement, the supreme leader

immediately reverted back to his fatherly soft tone and exclaimed, "wonderful! We shall begin the arrangements immediately. And I assure you, Avi, you have absolutely nothing to worry about. We are absolutely certain that the ritual will go according to plan and you will be welcomed back a hero, carrying the first child of a new epoch of peace!"

I forced myself to give the most powerful man in the world a smile. I was suddenly acutely aware of how under-dressed I was. They had made me feel so comfortable at the beginning of our talk, but now I knew they were the same as every other man I had ever met. They wanted something from me and would bargain, threaten and prob-ably even kill to get it from me. But, I realized I had no choice. I would rather take my chance with this warrior king than with fucking Bracken. With Bracken I knew what I was getting, at least the Zahothian would be some excitement, and who knows, maybe I would get a chance to escape.

"I will serve you proud," I almost gagged as I regurgi-tated the following, now meaningless, words: "supreme leader."

The old man walked over to the door and while putting on his coat theatrically exclaimed, "you are our savior Avi, you should be very proud."

He walked out the door and left me with the Nepharan who I, suddenly, felt quite fond of - at least he was not a human man.

"I have some essential equipment for you." He stated, as if he had not even witnessed the recent coercion.

He pulled out a loose leather bag from his robe and poured two items rather carelessly on the table. He revealed a rubber apparatus that looked a little like a translucent pig's ear, with a series of blinking lights shining through it and a small black case. I was pretty sure the pig's ear was a translator of some sort. I had seen visitors at the factory use them, but I had no idea about the other one.

The Nepharan picked up the case, opened it and pulled out a microscopic chip. He took out a little gun-type thingy out of his robe and placed the chip on the end of it. "This will twinge a little", he said as he zapped me on the neck with it.

"Ow! What the fuck?" I snarled at the alien.

"I said it would twinge," he said calmly.

"That is a tracking device which will allow us to monitor not only your location but your heart rate, adrenaline levels and other signs that may indicate danger. We will be with you the entire time."

"Reassuring," I answered a little more sardonically than I had intended. Luckily, the Nepharan did not seem to understand sarcasm very well and nodded at me with approval.

"The other items is less invasive." He picked up the transparent pig's ear and explained its function to me. As I suspected it was a translator that would allow me to understand the Zahothians. He showed me how to place it on my ear and I left it on.

The alien, then, having completed his business, arose and bid me farewell. He said that for the next couple of days before first contact, I would be entitled to all the hotel's services, however, I was not to leave the floor for my own safety. He would have a wardrobe sent to me posthaste (yes, he really used that word) and he would be there personally to take me to the rendezvous. It was weird. Even though I had been threatened not 10 minutes ago by the supreme leader, the presence of this alien made me feel safe and warm, and I truly appreciated his kindness. Even though he was as much a part of this barbaric process as the leader was.

Once he had left, I started to appreciate the gravity of the situation I was put in. If I did not do this, I would be sent back to that hellhole run by the monster Bracken. But was trading the monster you know for the monster you don't know the right choice? I had no answer. Something also seemed fishy about this entire situation. Why would they choose me for this important mission? I am literally nobody. Why not select someone with training? This whole thing seems to be put together at the last minute. We have had 100 years to prepare for the event and I am the best we can come up with? And what is with this alien poison? If this is so important for the future of our planet, why have they given me a weapon with which to kill the ambassador of a hostile alien race? There were no answers to these speculations. I was stuck in this guarded room whether I liked it or not. As a waiter brought in an extravagant plate of food which I was to understand was the breakfast, the supreme leader had sent for, I decided I would make the most of what were, presumably, my last days on earth.

Chapter Three

NEVAK

I OPENED MY EYES. Where was I? I seemed to be encased in some kind of glass cell. In horror, I noticed that I was suspended in a clear slime. I began to panic and struggle. I reached for my face and felt the shape of a mechanical octopus grasping my mouth. I thrashed harder and bashed my fists on the glass. I could not breathe. Suddenly, a loud noise above me and I gushed out of my prison onto the hard surface below with a painful bang. The slime seeped through the iron grids as I laid on the cold, hard floor. I still could not breathe and grasped the apparatus attached to my mouth and pulled it off. It is attached to a tube, at least a foot long, which I was forced to pull out of my throat. I gagged as I completed the procedure and finally the sweet release of breath overcame me as my lungs filled with air for what felt like the first time in years. I am still unable to remember what was happening to me or where I even was. I was still down on my knees covered in the goo I was imprisoned in and from this position I examined my surroundings. I seemed to be in some kind of hospital.

The walls of the large room were all a deep black with a slight red glow to them. In front of me there were four tables in a row, also black. I can only assume these were examination tables. They rose up from the floor as if part of the building. I saw a window but there was nothing outside, all I could see were stars beyond the blackness. I turned and gasped in horror as I noticed three more slime chambers with creatures just like me inside them. I felt a sharp tinge in my brain as I finally began to remember what was happening. I am Captain Nevak Drokhoggo of the planet Zahoth. I have been in cryogenic stasis for the past 2 years. This is my ship, the men in their hibernation chambers are my crew. I slowly picked myself up and stood on my two feet. I wobbled immediately and grasped one of the examination tables. I noticed that I was shivering violently along with my deep feeling of fatigue. Luckily, the examination table had a towel and a blanket on it. I grabbed the towel while still holding onto the table with one hand for balance and began to dry myself of the slime. This simple task seemed to activate something in my brain, and I remember that shivering and loss of muscle control are symptoms of awakening from long-term stasis. Memory loss and disillusionment are also common for the first few minutes after awakening. I sat myself on the table after drying myself off, more or less, and wrapped myself in the blanket in an attempt to get warm. After a few minutes, my shivering had become minimal and I could also remember more. We were headed to the planet earth (as named by the natives) in order to consolidate the shameful peace treaty signed by both planets one hundred years ago.

All of a sudden, I was overcome with a strong feeling

of frustration. This mission was a massive waste of time. The humans were a primitive people, unable of seeing the big picture. I was there 100 years ago. I saw their society and how they treated each other and their planet. The decision to invade a planet is not one taken lightly. I myself was unsure of the decision, but our scouts assured the council of elders that it was the best thing for the universe that we interfere in the earthlings' affairs. Unfortunately, the humans had advanced their technology to the point of mass destruction. This we did not find out until our first envoy ship was annihilated, before it could even establish contact with the humans, by missiles sent from multiple of their so-called nations. This was the largest casualty we had had in living memory. We had severely underestimated the brutality of the humans. As the information of the attack swept our planet, there was a strong sense of failure. How had we allowed this to happen? 137 Zahothian lives were lost in that attack and for the first time in a thousand years Zahoth went to war. The first thing we did was take out all of the nuclear weapon facilities. It was during this operation that we found out that this type of weapon was severely harmful to the planet and its inhabitants. I was shocked to discover that although over 100 Zahothian lives were lost in their attack. A further 10,000 human lives were lost due to radiation in the following weeks. How could the humans use such devices? Did they not understand the dangers? The humans celebrated their victory over us, but little did they know that a fleet was on its way from Zahoth.

Although all Zahothians are trained in the art of battle from an early age, it is always used a last resort. Our education process is extremely brutal, only 1/10 of our children survive to adulthood. But those who do become protectors of the universe. The humans clearly did not know who they were dealing with. Once the order came. One million of our soldiers set out to face these destructive primates. I among them. This time we would not send envoys. The attack would be swift and severe. It had become clear to the elders that the leaders of earth were unfit to rule. Full extermination was not the objective, but we were advised to hand out justice by any means necessary. Our warships were much more capable of withstanding the human defenses this time, and we landed on their planet 2 years after the initial act of aggression. Our objective was to destroy all military personnel and all weapons along with the ruling class. Our warriors were efficient, and this task only took us one earth moon cycle. The humans were extremely disorganized, as was expected, and were no match for us. All the million of us fought as one entity with no self-interest. Each casualty was felt by every one of us. The humans, on the other hand, showed no bravery in battle, and there were even some conflicts between human 'nations' during the conflict. It was unfathomable to me that a civilization that had come so far technologically had not progressed at all socially. It became clear that the humans' society relied on self-interest and oppression. It was an odd feeling going back there.

I shook off these memories and directed my attention to more urgent matters. I could feel my muscles becoming stronger and could now move my legs with ease, although accompanied by some pain. Having not used any of my muscles for the past two years had taken its toll. But, fortunately, this was only temporary and soon enough I should be back to my old self. I jumped off the table and walked over to the adjacent room. This is were we kept our gear for the duration of the trip. I dressed myself in my military uniform and continued over to the command module. I checked that we were still on course and that none of the ship's operations had malfunctioned. The entire vessel was controlled by AI, which made my job as captain relatively easy. There seemed to be a small decrease in pressure in engine room #2. Most likely a small pipe had ruptured or something similar. Nothing to worry about, but I should wake our engineer to investigate and repair any possible damage. We were still three earth days away from our destination. The captain of the ship always awoke first to secure the ship after a long stasis. Granted, two years was on the short side, but still quite significant, and there are no guarantees that the ship can maintain its course for that long, even with an advanced AI. However, everything seemed in order, so I decide to bring the rest of the crew out of their hibernation. I walk back to the lab containing the cryogenic stasis capsules and plant my thumb print on each of the screens attached to the capsules. This will begin the defrosting process, which can take up to an hour. I leave the lab and head to the kitchen in search of a nutrition pack. My appetite is awakening, that is a good sign.

As I devoured three ration packs in my post-stasis hunger. I started thinking about the mission that lay ahead. We were unable to monitor earth for the past century due to the interference by the Nepharans. Nephara - even thinking that name gives me the chills. They have been our enemies ever since the great bridging. Although you could not tell by looking at us, we began as the same species over 100 million years ago. It was not

until approximately 1 million years ago that our people
separated. The first king of the Zahothians Qrakhoro was
considered a great traitor on the planet known then as
Tanus. He led an insurgency against the ruling class who
had enslaved the majority of the population. Although
Qrakhoro had the numbers, the power of each side was
incredibly equal, due to the imbalance of technology and
military know-how. This struggle led to a war that lasted
for three generations. One of the unexpected advantages
of the long war was an acceleration of technological development. Finally, with the discovery of a hospitable planet
within range of our space technology, a truce was reached
and Qrakhoro, now an old man, would take all who wished
with him onto the new planet to start a new world. One
without a ruling class, one without injustice.

The migration took decades, and Qrakhoro would
never come to see the new world for which he had fought
so hard. But his legacy would be carried on, and he is still
honored as the first and only king of Zahoth. But, finally,
the fighting had ended, and our people could stop dying.
The new planet, which was named Zahoth, was harsh and
barren. The landscape was dominated by volcanoes and
magma. This was the only source of heat, it being so far
from the sun that temperatures were rarely over 0. The
life of the first settlers was short and miserable, but these
heroes laid the groundwork for the future of the greatest
planet in the universe. Within a few generations, Zahoth
became a prospering planet based on equality (the
meaning of the word 'Zahoth'). Due to the accelerated
need for space technology during the war, we now had the
capabilities to travel through the galaxies in search of life.
Unfortunately, so did the Nepharans. It turned out that

the Nepharans were not happy about the revolution and during the beginning stages of our society, launched multiple attacks in an attempt of revenge on the 'traitors.' However, our brave ancestors were able to fight them off and after a few centuries, these petty attacks stopped. Since this time both planets had gone their separate ways and were barely in contact with one another. Each of us still harbored a fierce resentment for the other, and this could be seen in our intergalactic dealings. Although, by now, each planet had become equal in military might and technology, their values could not be more different. No Zahothian has set foot on Nephara for over five hundred thousand years and returned to tell the tale. Same goes for Nepharans on Zahoth. We continue our eternal struggle among the stars, converting as many planets as we can to our way of life. We are the two counterweights of the universe and earth is our latest battleground.

Well, it is no longer a battleground. We relinquished our right to this planet when we signed the Nepharan peace treaty. Right before we had reached our objective in the battle. The Nepharans interfered in our mission. The humans would have been helpless without this aid from the stars. Once they joined forces with the humans, we had lost. The Nepharans supplied the humans with what is known on our planet as the 'bringer of decay.' The bomb is 100 times more powerful than the weapon used by the humans. Once detonated, it will kill anything within a 1000 mile radius and will leave the land scorched barren. No life can exist in the attacked area after it has been used. We do not know how they were able to establish contact with them to this day, but our mission was doomed the moment they did. I was leading a squadron through an especially brutal part of the world called Russia when I saw the cloud in the distance. We were immediately ordered to retreat, and it was not until we reached our ship that we learned that the weapon had killed 35% of our force in one blast. This was the largest casualty we had ever faced in the history of our planet. Our leaders immediately called a truce with the Nepharan and human leaders, to save the lives of the rest of our soldiers, and we left earth with the taste of death in our mouths.

We were forced to sign the ridiculous, humiliating treaty in order to save our troops still left on the ground. I did not ever think that I would return to this godforsaken place, and we had no idea what to expect upon our arrival on the hostile planet. The elders had considered not honoring the peace agreement due to the danger of the mission but, ultimately, it was decided that it was our duty to do so. Also, it was important to find out what had been happening on earth since our departure. The stipulation of interspecies mating was clearly the most outrageous. When Zahothians mate, we often injure our partners, and this is with the females of our planet who are almost as strong as the males. They go through the same training as we do, but unfortunately have a higher mortality rate, close to $1/50$ survive the training. Mating rituals take place publicly and are a great honor for those involved, but they can become violent. The male is unable to control himself when taken by the lust and often must be restrained by other males before killing the female. Furthermore, even if the mating ritual is successful, despite our advanced medicine, females often die in childbirth. For this reason, our population has been stable for the past one hundred thousand years. Consequently, we cannot afford to lose citizens to wars and tend to avoid them if at all possible. Our operation on earth was a massive hit to our planet, and we have been recovering from it ever since. Our elders believe this stipulation was put into the treaty in order to provoke a new conflict when the human female selected inevitably dies during the mating process. I had orders to gather as much intelligence as possible and harm no one as to not provoke the humans or the Nepharans. The Nepharans are master manipulators and have had millenniums of practice, we would have to be on our guard for the entire duration of our stay.

We had learned from last time that bringing a large force to earth will result in immediate attack, even if the force has peaceful intentions, so this time, the elders decided on no more than a small squad to carry out the mission and report back with intelligence. An hour had surely passed by now, although my sense of time was still a little shaky. Therefore, I made my way back into the lab to check on my team. Rokha and Chavak were each sitting on a hospital bed looking very pale, but Qroko was still in his chamber. I rushed over to check his vital signs on the hibernation monitor. His heart rate had barely risen since I pushed the release button. This was not looking good. Cryogenic stasis carried its risks, we all knew that, and there were multiple reasons someone might not awake from hibernation, too many to list. Despite his heart rate still being extremely slow, his other vital signs seemed to be in order. It is possible there was nothing wrong with him but something wrong with the stasis chamber. If this was the case, we would be unable to fix it until we got back to Zahoth. Poking around in there would most likely do more harm than good, even if it was done by an experienced engineer like Rokha. I double-checked Qroko's vital signs and confirmed that the best plan of action was to do nothing. He could be taken out of stasis safely back home. This setback put me in a somber mood. Qroko was my number two, he was my chief intelligence officer; we had fought together many times, and he was my oldest friend. Before being deployed on this mission, Chavak, Qroko, and I had been on a two-year long planet hopping mission searching for intelligent life. We had come up with nothing during this time and as one of the closest ships to earth were called for this mission. Rockha had been stationed alone on a planet containing intelligent life, due to the fact that the inhabitants were so physically small it was decided that even one more of us giants would have scared them too much. As far as I knew, he had spent 10 years there and did not seem very happy to be leaving. However, he seemed to be a proficient soldier and engineer, which is all one could ask for. Our former engineer was killed on a hostile planet by what I can only describe as a monster. We had just disembarked our spacecraft when an entire flock of these armor-plated beasts stampeded through our ranks. Our engineer was trampled to death immediately and there was something we could do. For this reason, Rockha was added to my crew. Chavak was a young soldier with little experience, but he had proven himself in combat and was somewhat of a prodigy in medicine and will most certainly come in handy if things go wrong.

Next, I turned my attention to my other two men. They were both still clearly feeling the effects of the stasis. I picked up their gear and brought it to them so that they would not have to make the trek to the adjacent room.

They both gave a lazy nod as I laid their clothes down next to them. They would not be capable of having a conversation for another hour or so. I did a quick examination of both of them and determined that all was well. I told them to come meet me in the kitchen when they had the strength. Both nodded, seeming to understand my instructions. They would start feeling hungry in a little while, so I walked back to the kitchen and prepared some ration packs for them. I left them three each on the dining table and walked back to the command module. I was feeling like myself once again, apart from a ferocious sense of dread. I could see a shape in the distance through the glass, it was a tiny speck, but I knew that was where we were headed. We would be arriving soon, and we had no idea what was waiting for us there.

Chapter Four
AVI

IF IT WASN'T for the crippling anxiety I was feeling in anticipation of being fucked to death by a fierce alien warrior, the last two days would have been some of the best in my life. I ate like an absolute pig. I had never known such abundance. I swear, every time a waiter came in with room service the guards would look at me in disgust. But I could not care less. The platters were always packed with most decadent delicacies our planet had to offer. I could not believe that places like this existed. I had never even sampled most of the foods on the menu. All I knew was rye porridge, bread, the occasional fruit and synthetic meat, but we weren't even allowed to have the good stuff, even though we were the ones carrying our economy. When I was not eating, I was in the spa area on my floor. The entire place had been cleared out for me. I used the sauna at least twice a day. As well as the jacuzzi and swimming pool. Also, they have this drink called champagne that is simply excellent. I have gone through a few bottles a day and let me tell you, a couple of glasses of that, and you will completely forget every negative thought.

Unfortunately, the champagne had now worn off, and it was the morning of the meetup with the alien ambassador. All of a sudden, I felt like absolute shit. My head was pounding, I was incredibly thirsty, and I felt pretty close to throwing up. I hungrily reached over for a glass on the nightstand and gulped down the fluid. I spit it out immediately and ran to the marble-covered bathroom and puked my guts out in the fancy toilet bowl. Champagne tasted amazing yesterday, but I guess it was not a morning drink. I wiped my mouth off and walked back to the bed and crashed down on to the soft heaven. The clock showed 09:27. I was told, more like ordered, to be ready at 10:00. The clothes they had provided me with were odd to say the least. It was a robe much like the Nepharan had been wearing, but there was a little slit in the front so my legs were visible. I guess they had tried to make me look sexy to the alien. I had tried it on the night before and thought I looked like a festive tampon. But, I guess that was the fashion on planet Zahoth.

Physically I already felt much better but, unfortunately, this now allowed me to concentrate on my mental and emotional state and there was not much good that could be said about those. I was simultaneously glad that I was out of the hands of that sadistic loser Bracken. On the other hand, I felt like a prisoner marching towards the electric chair. They say that the anticipation of death is much worse than death itself, however, in my case, I don't think this applies. No one that I know of has been raped and murdered by an intergalactic beast. The singular upside in my situation suddenly starts to feel pretty insignificant. I take another, more careful swig of champagne and fill up the glass. Turns out it is a morning drink after all, I say to myself as I down the flute.

By the time the Nepharan arrived to pick me up, I had managed to make myself look reasonably presentable and was also quite tipsy from the drink. He greeted me with that robotic wave as he stepped into the room and asked, "are you ready to go, Avi 2564?"

I gave him a solemn nod and walked over to the door. He held it open and allowed me to lead us into the elevator, the two guards right on our heels. Once we got down into the hotel lobby, I saw that there was a massive crowd outside. I asked my alien companion what was going on.

"They are here to see you, of course," he answered wholesomely.

I was taken aback by this answer. I had been under the impression that this was a secret operation, but it turns out hundreds of people had turned up to watch the lamb of humanity get taken to slaughter. Somehow the people made this whole thing feel even less real. It was like I was the only real person here, everyone else was just pretending. I walked along the path surrounded by a sea of people waving and chanting. All the faces seemed like masks. Everyone was dressed in a standard issue suit, which further enhanced my feeling of separation from the world considering what I was wearing. All the faces just became a single mass, and it felt like a force was carrying me forward. By the time we got into the hover vehicle, I could not even remember whether they were happy or sad to see me.

There was something about my alien companion that felt odd. I had no reason to feel warmly towards him, but i was overwhelmed with a sense of trust in him. His presence had an anaesthetizing effect on me. For the entire trip out of the city, I felt like I was just going through the motions. It was not until we had left the maze of skyscrapers that I finally saw the ship and awoke from my trance. Time had lost its meaning, so I did not know how long we had travelled, but we were certainly not in the city anymore. We were now in a forest with large dark trees towering over us. I had never seen trees this big since the landscape in my district was completely flat. The ship was nowhere near as impressive as I had thought an alien ship would be. In our history books, we had had drawings of the Zahothian ships and they looked massive and terrifying. This seemed like the alien version of a rowboat. The ship itself was a matte black with red glowing veins all around it, it almost looked like a living organism rather than a transportation vessel, and could be mistaken for a kind of alien wasp. As we drew closer, I could make out a small hatch slowly opening. My heart began pounding even harder. This was where I would enter into my new life. Would I ever be the same again? Would I ever even get to leave this place or was I entering my grave?

The Nepharan gave me a signal to activate my translator by pressing the small button on the side. I raised my hand to my ear and pushed it. I felt a strange tingle in my brain as it activated. I took a deep nervous breath and one last look out the back of our vehicle, at the luminescent city in the distance as our vehicle entered the alien vessel.

We flew into a chamber which looked much like the outside of the ship. It was all black except for the glowing red veins throughout. It was like they were pulsing blood through them. It made me feel eerie, like I had been eaten by a giant creature. We stepped out of the vehicle. I could now feel my hands shaking and legs almost buckling. The chamber was large with a ceiling at least 50 feet high and otherwise empty except for a large door at the end of it. I kept close to my alien companion since he had instructed our guards to stay in the vehicle. I was unable to control my gaze, looking every which way in curiosity. I was inside an alien ship. This was insane.

Suddenly, we heard a loud creak or maybe more of a puff. I grabbed the Nepharan's arm in fright as the door about 20 feet from us was slowly opening. The wait felt excruciatingly long, and I could hardly hide my anticipation and fear as to what we were about to see. However, the Nepharan seemed completely at ease, which calmed me somewhat. The door had clearly not been opened in some time since there was a cloud of dust in front of the entrance. Finally, I saw a single figure pacing through the dust. I could only see its outline, but it looked massive. As the dust cleared, I got a better look at what we were facing. The figure was at least 8 feet tall and completely hairless apart from light-colored eyebrows. Its skin was translucent, I could almost see through it, but as the dust cleared I could detect a slight blue color. The eyes of the creature were a smouldering black. The most confusing thing was how much it looked like a human. As the creature approached with its relaxed yet determined gait, I could see how muscular it was. Even with its slight translucence, I could make out every muscle in its body. All it was wearing was a loin cloth reminding me of a primitive sort of Scottish kilt as well as a skin tight sash around its upper body. The sash had multiple markings on it in a language could not understand. I assumed these were our equivalent of military medals. Its arms were covered in tattoos going all the way up to the pecs, and they seemed to glitter in the low infrared light of the chamber. I stood completely still, in awe of what my eyes were beholding. This was not at all what I had expected. I thought they would look more like the Nepharans with their almost bird-like figure attached to a squiddy head. In some way I could see the resemblance in the two, but I could not quite understand what it was exactly. The Zahothian ambassador certainly looked nothing like the Zahothians in our text books. There, they were depicted as lizard-type creatures with hideous fangs and sharp claws. If it wasn't for the circumstances, I could see myself being attracted to this thing.

The alien stopped about five feet in front of us and assumed a strong, masculine stance. He stated something in a booming voice that I could not understand. Clearly, my translator was not working, I went to fiddle with it but the Nepharan touched my hand and said in clear English to the alien, "we may talk in Zahoth, the human's translator is calibrated to understand you."

The ambassador nodded and proceeded in his mother tongue rather than what I assume was Nepharan a few moments ago. "Greetings, it is my great honor to be a part of the melding of our two species."

There was a long pause. The Nepharan gently nudged me. "Oh, yes, the honor is all mine," I answered abruptly. This whole thing was fucking ludicrous. Here I was talking about honor while I was literally being handed over to an alien for procreation. The problem was that the situation was so absurd that the least ridiculous course of action seemed to be to play along with the proceedings.

The alien nodded at me gently and turned his attention to the Nepharan. "And who, may I ask, are you?" he asked with an ounce of suspicion in his voice.

"Of course, my manners. My name is Ormen Askan, high chancellor of foreign affairs of the united planets of Nephara. How do you do?"

"That's quite a mouthful. Do tell me what a high chancellor is doing all the way out here on earth? Don't you have other planets to enslave?"

The Nepharan's face did not flinch, "if by enslave, you mean protect, then certainly, but unlike you savages, we value every life in the universe.

"Oh, do you now? How about the life of this poor girl? You know as well as I do that interspecies mating is impossible between our two races."

I looked up at the Nepharan perplexed. Was this true? If it was, then why I even here?

"I know nothing of the sort. We are certain that the mating ritual will go as planned." The Nepharan countered, face still frozen.

"Cut the crap, we both know what's going on here. I don't even know why you bother with this treaty. I will venture a guess, the population of earth is what, say 10 billion by now?"

I interrupted in anger, "try 3 billion, thanks to you."

The Zahothian looked at me deep black eyes widened, "3 billion, that's impossible" it said in disbelief.

"That's what happens when you kill 5 billion people, takes some time to bounce back." I continued with aggression.

The Zahothian was no longer looking at me and turned his attention back to my companion. "You monsters, all those lives for some fucking Barnox."

"We just finished what you started, Khlopya," the Nepharan said, kind of menacingly.

The Zahothian took a step forward and asked angrily, "what the fuck did you just call me?"

I noticed his skin gradually transforming color from a light blue to an intense red. I was more than confused. I no longer had any idea what they were talking about. What is Barnox? And what did my companion say to make him angry?

"Calm yourself, savage. If you touch me, the treaty is void. I have the entire empire of Nephara behind me."

The Zahothian was breathing heavily. His mighty chest heaving as he tried to calm himself. Slowly his breath turned to normal, but his complexion remained a dark red. He was now standing uncomfortably close to us, and I felt myself trembling at the size and stature of this alien warrior towering over me. The Nepharan matched the Zahothian in height but would surely have no chance in a fight due to their difference in size and definition.

The Zahothian closed his eyes, took a long deep breath and said in half a whisper, "down with rulers." Then in one swift move, he drew a blade from under his cloth and sliced the Nepharan's head clean off. The decapitated body fell to its knees almost in slow motion as my brain attempted to process what had just happened. Finally, my companion collapsed on the floor, his head rolling a few feet from where we were standing. A flow of blood was gushing from the neck of the falling alien. The Zahothian was now a deep burning red like what I imagined the color of hell to be. He pushed me with his left hand and I flew into the wall and collapsed to the floor. I saw him hesitate and look down at me before drawing his weapon and shooting both guards in the head with two precise shots through the windshield with some kind of space weapon. The speed with which he moved was incredible.

I reached up and touched the back of my head; I looked at my hand covered in blood and the room went black.

Chapter Five

NEVAK

FUCKING NEPHARAN SHOULD HAVE KEPT his mouth shut and none of this would have happened. The entitlement of that race never seizes to astound me. It has been half a mega-annum since our species divided and he still has the audacity to call me 'khlopya.' But that was just the icing on the cake. The real reason I did what I did was due to the monstrous revelation about what had happened on earth since we left. We knew the Nepharans were bad, but this was downright evil. They had no right to be doing what they are doing and who else was going to stop them. The humans are completely helpless. Zahoth is the one true protector of the universe and its time we started acting like it. My crew did not feel quite as strongly as I did.

"You did what!?" Rockha exclaimed as I told him what happened.

"And what in Qrakhoro's name is this!?" he continued with the same level of intensity while pointing his finger at the human I held in my arms.

"I couldn't just leave her, could I?" I said.

"Yes. You could have. Do you realize what this means?" Rockha cut me off before I could answer, "this means war and not just some little battle like on earth, this means war with Nephara. Do you have any idea what you have started?"

"You don't understand Rockha... what the Nepharan's have done, it's... it's..."

"I don't give a fuck what they have done. You have just single-handedly doomed our planet."

Rockha was getting more and more heated as he continued, I could see the rage rising in him. Chavak stepped in, "there's no point fighting about this, what's done is done. And Rockha, you forget your place, this is our captain you are speaking to."

Rockha protested, but Chavak cut him off, "what are your orders, captain?"

"This human needs medical attention, please see to her Chavak, and thank you."

"Yes, sir," Chavak answered and took the girl in his arms.

"This is absurd!" Rockha exclaimed.

"Never mind about the damn human, we need to notify the elders, the Nepharans could be on their way to attack as we speak."

"They will not do that, Rockha," I said calmly, hoping that my peaceful manner would be contagious.

"They probably do not even know what has happened yet, Rockha, how could they?" Chavak intervened, the human female now in his hands.

"I knew we should have come with you, you can't be trusted with matters as important as this."

"Rockha, that is enough," I snapped.

"Go and cool off and we can discuss what to do about the situation."

Rockha looked at both me and Chavak in dismay and said, "unbelievable," and stormed off brushing my shoulder as he left. I did not have time to think about Rockha, there were more pressing matters.

"Can you help her, Chavak?"

"I will do my best, I may need some assistance, please accompany me to the lab."

Chavak led us into the lab and placed the human on one of the examination tables. As he laid her down for the second time today, I was struck by this odd feeling. There was something so soft and vulnerable about the way she looked. I found myself examining her with my gaze meticulously. Her light wavy hair came down past over her soft-featured face leading to her plump breasts. Last time on earth, I had noted the curves of the human female, however, now, up this close, I could truly appreciate the form. It was not just her breasts, her waist and hips were much fuller than the females of my planet, and something about this ignited a fire inside me. I was not really sure what was happening. Was I attracted to this human? I do not see how that was possible, but I have no other explanation.

I snapped out of my infatuation as I remembered what I had done to put her in this position. When I pushed her, I was attempting to shield her from the possible resistance from the guards if I was to miss. It was not my intention to push her so hard that she hit the wall. I had forgotten how dainty and light the humans were. A push like that on a Zahothian would have barely knocked her down. I felt terrible that I had endangered an innocent.

Chavak went to work on her head, and luckily for me, the cut was not very big. It took him no time to have it patched up. Fortunately, human anatomy is relatively similar to our own despite the differences in size, strength, and appearance.

"Ok, that should do it," Chavak said with a sigh of relief. "What now?" he continued.

That really was a good question. What now? The adrenaline was slowly disappearing, and I was beginning to face the harsh reality I had created for us head on. I had disobeyed a direct order from the elders and jeopardized my men. There was no point dithering though. In my decades of military experience, the most valuable lesson I had learned was to not waste one's time with regrets. What was done was done. Now, I needed to adapt to the situation as efficiently as I possibly could. I weighed the options in my head. As far as I could tell, we had two. Cut and run or own up to what had happened. If we were to go down and tell the humans and their Nepharan overlords that I had killed two guards and a high-ranking Nepharan official I do not think any of us would be getting back home alive. The first option sounded simple. It could be hours if not a full day until the Nepharans would confirm exactly what had happened here. That is quite a nice head start if we were to make our escape. However, even if we were to survive, my reckless actions would most likely result in further deaths of my people. Also, what the hell were we going to do about this human on board? I could not very well return her to earth, they might think she had something to do with it. Hell, I did not even know who she was. For all I know, she was a soldier undercover. I needed more information before I could decide what to do.

"I need to talk to the human, when do you think she will be conscious?"

"I would imagine very soon. I do not think she has a concussion. I would suggest letting her lie down for a while before attempting to wake her."

"Agreed."

I led Chavak out of the room and told him I would get back to him with a plan as soon as possible. He reluctantly left the room after I explained that another alien presence might be too much of a shock for the human. She had already seen me, so I hoped that maybe she would not overreact when she finally woke up.

Chapter Six

AVI

OH SHIT, not again. This is the second time in the past week I had woken up and not recognized where the hell I was. I laid completely still, staring at the weird-looking light shining down on me. It was blinding, and my eyes were adjusting much slower than usual. I was straining them constantly, trying to figure out where I was. Finally, I began to see the outline of the room I was in. It looked a little like a hospital, but not any hospital I had ever seen. All the machinery was really weird. As I turned my head to examine the left side of the room, I screamed in horror. It was the fucking alien! The Zahothian ambassador... who had just massacred my entourage. He was standing on the other side of the room and seemed to be in thought. His face looked pensive, almost sad. But what did I know, as far as my knowledge of alien warrior races goes, he might have been smiling. Suddenly, his gaze met mine, and I turned my head rapidly back to its former position, but the damage was done, the monster had seen me.

He stepped towards me and I immediately shot up into

a sitting position on my hard alien bed and shouted, "get the fuck away from me!"

Surprisingly, he did actually stop, and put his hands up as what I can only assume was his version of 'I come in peace.'

His reaction surprised me and I had not really planned my actions much further. I did not know my next step.

"Where am I?" I demanded in my harshest voice.

"You are on my ship." The Zahothian answered calmly.

I guess that should have been obvious considering the last thing I could remember was arriving on his ship. "Why did you kill those people and attack me?"

He looked down seriously in reaction to my question. "It is complicated... I do not have time to explain it to you right now. I need to talk to you. I promise that I will not hurt you if you please just calm down."

"Calm down!? How could I possibly be calm? I just saw you murder three people and you are asking me to stay calm. For all I know, I'm next on your list. You already attacked me during the meeting. What the fuck was that about?"

"If I wanted to kill you, human, then I would have done so already. I have no intention of harming you. I was attempting to shield you earlier. I am sorry for causing you pain. I simply need some information and you will be returned to your planet."

His calm way of speaking had a similar effect on me and I felt much better than I did a minute ago and I was willing to do anything to get out of here, so I took a deep breath and said, "Ok, ask your questions, but this is all still completely fucked up, you realize that, right?"

He ignored my last comment and immediately dived into his first question, "who are you?"

Before I could answer this incredibly vague inquiry, he specified, "I mean, why were you selected for this mission. What are you, military?

"No, I work in a mine, I am nobody."

He made a strange puffing noise. It was kind of cute and retorted, "that is not possible. Why would they send you here?"

"Hey, buddy, I've been asking the same question this whole time. Apparently I won some kind of lottery or something, so call me miss lucky."

"That does not make any sense," the Zahothian answered, looking confused. He began pacing in front of me with his hand rubbing his chin. He really did look like a human, just one much more physically advanced. I was now able to fully appreciate his body up close. There was no way in hell I was going to act on my attraction. The guy was clearly a murdering psycho, but I did believe he was not going to harm me. So there was no harm in looking while he pondered. I did not really understand what he was thinking about, anyway. He clearly knew something I didn't.

"Who sent you here? The Nepharan yes, but who else?"

"The supreme leader of earth."

He looked pensive again and seemed to be thinking hard. "Did they give you anything, I mean, other than your translator?"

"No, nothing," I lied, deciding not to mention the tracking chip.

"I cannot understand this. What possible motive

would the Nepharans have of giving a complete nobody over to me. If you were someone important, I would understand it. You dying would cause an uproar, but no one will miss you."

"A little harsh," I said indignantly.

"No, that is not what I mean. I just mean that if they wanted to start a war, they would have sent someone else."

"Why would they want to start a war? You are the ones who invaded us. We just want you to leave us alone. You are the ones who created this insane peace treaty in the first place."

"You have been fed a million lies throughout your life, human. You have no idea what happened on this planet 100 years ago. Zahothians do not just butcher the population of an entire planet. We are the guardians of equality in the universe."

"Guardians of equality?" I scoffed. "I literally just saw you murder that Nepharan and he was nothing but nice to me and what about those guards? You killed them without a second thought."

"Your 'mind had been twisted human. Presumably the minds of all earthlings have. I will tell you what I believe is happening. I am not completely certain on all the details, but it is the only narrative that makes any sense." He paused and took a deep breath. I was now on the edge of the table, waiting eagerly for what he had to say. I was not sure I trusted him, but he seemed genuinely troubled and sincere, so I thought it was only fair that I at least heard him out.

"102 earth years ago, a scouting party from our planet was sent into your orbit to make first contact with the newly discovered planet. This planet. It was shot down almost immediately by a powerful bomb that we now know to be one which utilized nuclear power. A primitive weapon, but certainly powerful. The entire party was killed in the unprovoked attack. However, they had been able to send back intelligence before this happened. We discovered that the planet was divided into areas you call nations and each nation was governed by a separate ruling class. The degree of oppression varied by nation, but it was present throughout the planet. Our elders decided that the only way to restore equality among humans would be to eliminate the ruling class completely. A force was sent to your planet to do so."

"But you didn't just kill the ruling class, you killed so many innocent people." I interjected.

"No, we did not!" the Zahothian retorted angrily, smashing his fist on to the table. His skin had turned red once again, which scared me and put me back on edge.

"I'm sorry, I didn't mean to..."

The Zahothian cut me off, returning to his pale blue color, "No, I am sorry, you don't know any better. I should not get angry with you. Just, please, hear the end of what I have to tell you."

I gave a single deep nod, and he continued, "we did not want to take any chances with a species as openly hostile as yours so the force sent was large. Almost one million Zahothian soldiers in one thousand ships. At first, we thought the sheer presence of our fleet would persuade the rulers into relinquishing their power, but we were mistaken. Not a single nation folded, and we were forced to attack. We could not risk killing innocents, so the attack was carried out by squadrons in hand to hand combat. We made light work of your military and were sweeping the land clean of the oppressive scum that ruled you. We had liberated nearly every nation when the Nepharans intervened."

"So, wait, you're saying that you did not kill any civilians?"

"That is correct. We would never harm innocent people, they were to be the future of earth."

"But then what happened to our population?"

"I am not completely sure, but I have a theory. The Nepharans supplied your largest nation with a weapon. A truly destructive one that, as far as we know, has never been used before due to the sheer magnitude of the destruction it reaps. The weapon kills all life and turns wherever it explodes into a barren wasteland for millennia. The weapon was dropped on our main camp with the use of Nepharan ships. We did not see the attack coming and until that moment were unaware of the Nepharans' presence in the conflict. It wiped out over a third of our army and we were forced to retreat. We were forced to sign the ridiculous treaty under duress and were banished from earth for the next 100 years in exchange for the rest of our soldiers. My heart ached for the people of your planet as we packed up and left, leaving you to your new overlords. But we had no choice. We could not lose more soldiers or our home planet would have been left vulnerable to attack.

I stared at the Zahothian in astonishment, "we had been told that the peace treaty was made by Zahoth and that you had forced these terms upon us."

"I thought as much. I believe that after we left, the nation the Nepharans had selected to do their bidding led the planet into a civil war. With the weapons at their disposal it would have hardly been a war though, more like an extermination. In addition, we had already crippled most of the militaries and ruling classes of earth and left them helpless. If we had been allowed to complete our mission, we would have stayed to help you rebuild a fair and just society based on equality and planetary brotherhood, but instead we helped the new reign of terror sweep your planet."

"But why would anyone want to exterminate their own people? What did they get out of it?"

"I think the humans were under the influence of the Nepharans. When I said the weapon is not used. I meant that it is not used as a weapon. It is used by the Nepharans for mining purposes. When you told me that you worked in a mine, I realised why the Nepharans interfered in our mission. I believe that under earth's surface there is an unlimited supply of Barnox. This is the substance that powers the entire planet of Nephara. It is extremely powerful and with the right technology can be used for just about anything. Nepharans exhausted their own supply a long time ago and ever since have been planet hopping searching for it in order to keep their disgusting society running. This was the first time that our interests have clashed and we lost."

"But, all we mine is Bridgmanite. It's basically a rock."

"Exactly, have you never wondered why you do it?"

"Well, we were told it used to construct buildings."

"How many buildings did you see built of that on your way to my ship."

I paused for a second. Oh my god, was I really this stupid. I had never even questioned the stories fed to me. Why would they use that piece of shit rock for building? It basically crumbled in your hands. "No, not one. God, I feel like an idiot" I said.

"You are not an idiot you have been fed propaganda from your earliest days. It is incredibly difficult to break out of that kind of mental prison. It is likely everything you have known has been a lie. The Nepharans will go to any lengths to obtain this substance and earth, it seems, is an important source.

I felt my world come crashing down as he continued talking. My entire life was a lie. "Please, continue, what happened on earth after you left?"

"I do not wish to shock you further. I can tell that what I am saying is disturbing you." He moved towards me and touched my shoulder as tears came to my eyes. His touch felt warm and comforting. For some reason, him being here made hearing all this bearable. I wiped my eyes with my hands and urged him to continue, assuring him that I am ok and that I have to know the truth.

"Ok, as you wish. It is my belief that once we had left earth the Nepharans, using this powerful nation to do their bidding, proceeded to bomb vast areas of earth's surface. I do not believe they would have cared about any human life lost in the process. This would account for the drastic drop in your population. The survivors of the other nations were turned into slaves and made to harvest the crop that the Nepharans crave. You have not told me everything about your life, but I imagine a cover story was then created where we, the Zahothians, were portrayed as a great evil and the Nepharans as your saviors. This lie along with strict oppression of the lower working class allowed for the complete enslavement of the entire planet."

"But, we often see videos and pictures from all around the world. Our planet stands for peace and prosperity. We must work in the mines to develop our planet."

"These are all lies. I estimate that the ruling class of your planet is less than 1% of the population and the rest are slaves. But even the ruling class are not free, they are controlled by the Nepharans. Not all would work in the mines as the planet needs to run, but the vast majority are just like you. And have most likely been told lies just like you. Your planet has been enslaved by and advanced evil race and your own nature, driven by greed and selfishness. I am certain you felt the effect of the Nepharan's presence on your way here. They have influenced technology way beyond our grasp and they use it shamelessly on lower life forms."

I was now sobbing uncontrollably. I was sure everything he was saying was true. It made perfect sense. If he was the monster that I had been told he was, then why would he be treating me so kindly? Why had I been forced to work in the mines since I was 12 years old? What planet based on unification would do that?

The Zahothian put his arm around me and I pushed my face into his hard tattooed chest. "I know, human, it is difficult to hear this, but it is the truth."

"I know, I believe you," I answered through sobs. "My name is Avi, by the way," I said, not wanting to be called 'human' any longer it felt so cold and detached. I just wanted someone to hold me. My life on earth had been a hard one, and I hated my superiors and, to be honest, I did not even make many friends among the underlings, but finding out that it was all a lie was both a relief as well as devastating. I was relieved that I was not a descendant of a traitor against humanity and that I had been falsely led to believe that I was inferior to fellow humans, but I wept for my planet. All those people - slaves - were down there and no one was going to help them. They would spend the rest of their lives mining for that fucking rock for their alien overlords, and they would have no idea. I turned my head and looked up at the handsome alien liberator and felt such affection for him. He had saved me from a life of slavery. He pulled me in tighter and looked down on me with his strong, manly features and deep black eyes, it was like there was an entire universe in the depths of those beautiful spheres. Without quite knowing what I was doing, I leaned up and kissed his soft lips. He did not pull away. On the contrary, he kissed me back with force. I could feel his coarse tongue on the precipice of my mouth as we embraced in the first kiss between our people. He laid me down on the table and covered me with his warm, muscular body. He began kissing my neck as I moaned in pleasure. There was something electric about his touch. Whenever he laid his lips on me, I felt these micro-orgasms in my pussy emanating from that spot. It was like every touch sent a bolt of pleasurable lightning into my panties. I dug my fingers into his muscular back as he continued further down towards my breasts. Suddenly, he ripped off my robe. He split the cloth in two with ease and began sucking on my now rock hard nipples while he massaged my tits with his strong hands. He was firm but gentle in his actions. I moaned as his tongue flicked my nipple with great speed and skill, I was already moaning hard and could not wait to have this alien warrior inside me. But, suddenly, he stopped what he was doing and pulled away. I could see he was going through an inner battle. His eyes were telling me he wanted me but it seemed like he was fighting the urge to take me.

"What's wrong, Nevak?" I asked in a supportive tone. He had shown me nothing but kindness, and I wanted to return the favor.

"We cannot do this," he said solemnly, lowering his head.

"Don't you want me?" I asked vulnerably.

"That's not the issue, Avi. If we continue, I will hurt you, I most likely will kill you. My species is not made for sex. I am programmed to furiously plant my seed in the female with no regard for her safety. I will be unable to control myself, if we go any further and although, in this moment, I know that I would never hurt you, when in heat, I cannot make that promise."

My heart sank. The things I was feeling for this guy, alien, whatever, were real and I had never felt this way about a man before. I could not believe that I would never get to have him completely.

"Is there nothing, we can do? We can go as slow as you like and if you feel..." he cut me off with a shake of his head, "no, once I reach a certain point, nothing will stop me. This was the Nepharans' plan all along. You were never meant to survive, Avi. They were going to have me kill you and then kill me to provoke an attack from Zahoth. You being killed would get the underlings on side and willing to fight, and once Zahoth invaded they would have another excuse for the next century. The foundation for terror does not last forever, it needs to be renewed. Even if Zahoth was not provoked into an attack by my death, then your death would have unified the lower classes in a hatred of Zahothians. Your government could then, in the name of security, oppress its population even harder. There is nothing that can be done."

"But, we can't just leave everyone here to be slaves!" I retorted angrily.

"There is nothing to be done, human. You and I cannot be together and there is nothing we can do to help earth. I am sorry."

"Some guardians of the universe you are!" I yelled while bouncing off the table to confront Nevak.

"I thought you cared about us, about me, but you don't give a shit. You're just like every other guy I've ever met, aren't you?"

Nevak said nothing in response and bowed his head, "I know you are angry, but this is my decision. For your own safety, I will lock you in my quarters while we decide what to do. Hopefully, this will give you some time to calm down."

"Fuck calming down! Let me off this damn ship right now, I don't want anything to do with you!" is screamed at Nevak through my tears.

"If I release you, they will kill you. If you survive, then this has all been for nothing."

"I would rather die than stay here with you," I answered harshly.

I thought for a moment that I saw Nevak's eyes water up before he hoisted me up onto his shoulder with ease and carried me down the corridor to his quarters. I struggled the whole way pounding the back of the warrior furiously but he did not even react to my attempts to free myself from his grip. He placed me on his bed and told me he would be back for me shortly with a plan.

"Go to hell," I said spitefully as he closed the door.

I buried my face in his pillow and sobbed uncontrollably. I did not know what to do. The only thing I wanted
was for Nevak to walk back in and comfort me, but I knew
that was not going to happen. We could not be together, it
was impossible. I don't know why I had fallen so strongly
for an alien I barely knew. But I could already see that he
was the best man I had ever met. Honorable, strong, and
honest. I had just found out that my entire life was a lie
why was I not allowed the tiniest bit of comfort in the
form of an alien guardian. It was like a cruel cosmic joke.
There was nothing to be done though, all I could do was
await Nevak's decision and I could not see an option
where I would not be royally fucked.

Chapter Seven

NEVAK

WHAT THE FUCK was happening to me? Why did I care so much about this earthling? I have never been so close to reaching heat. How could I let myself be so stupid? Her gorgeous face, her voluptuous curves, her intoxicating scent, I could not get her out of my head. The moment she laid her head on my chest, my dick had woken up from its slumber. I had never used it before; I had no interest in killing someone, no matter what race they are. I had never felt such attraction to anyone of my own race before. Why was this different? It was like a warm liquid was filling up my body, I would almost lose myself in the lovely sensation and then logic would remind me that I could never indulge in the way she made me feel. I could never be her mate. I had traveled the stars for over 150 years and not once had I felt this way. 150 years relatively, of course. I had done so many space jumps and stints of cryogenic stasis that although I was no more than 30 years (43 earth years) old; I had seen my planet and others go through decades. This was the sacrifice we made as guardians of the universe, and

I was honored to be a part of it. However, it did get lonely. I had seen many planets, and many of them had families and couples living in harmony. I had always dreamed that would be me one day, but that was not how Zahothians were born. We did not know this mysterious entity called 'love' on earth. Every planet had a different name for it, but we Zahothians have never been able to comprehend its meaning. I have been told that it is not something you can explain. You just have to feel it. And I wish to feel it more than anything. I wish to know what it is like to have a partner. Someone who supports you in everything you do, someone who is always there for you. But, alas, these hopes are futile. I am doomed to travel the stars alone, the only comfort I have being my duty to every form of life.

At the moment, that felt like a cold comfort. I was rushing back to the command module to discuss our plan of action with the crew. I had all but decided that we were to get off this planet as quickly as possible and report back to the elders, but in the name of equality, I wanted to run it by my crew. Rockha, especially, was concerning me greatly. I was not sure how he would take the news.

With the touch of my finger to the screen, the command module door slid open and I walked in on a heated discussion between my men. Rockha was in Chavak's face, screaming in a fit of rage. I barged in and separated the two.

"What is the meaning of this?" I demanded from both of them.

Rockha's veins were bulging as he panted and gave me an angry answer, "Chavak, here thinks we should flee and take the alien female with us."

I looked over at Chavak, who was much calmer than

Rockha, and turning back to Rockha said, "I agree with him. That seems to be our only course of action. It is only a matter of time before the Nepaharans discover what has happened and we are all dead. Furthermore, we cannot just leave the human here. She will be killed."

"That's ridiculous. Why would the humans kill one of their own?" Rockha snapped.

I proceeded to explain what I had figured out about earth with the help of Avi. They both gasped in horror as I related the grizzly details of the fate of planet earth since the Zahothian fleet left its atmosphere.

"That is truly horrifying, we must help the humans," Chavak said compassionately.

Rockha's reaction was different. He was deadly afraid of the Nepharans and quickly suggested that we return the female and leave the planet to handle its own matters. I was shocked at Rockha's lack of empathy.

"May I remind you, Sergeant Rockha, that you have sworn an oath to protect every living being in this universe from the forces of corruption and evil."

"Yes, but..."

"There are no 'buts,' Sergeant, we have a duty to protect this human and we will do that duty."

"If we simply return this human to the Nepharans, we can absolve ourselves of the entire situation. They will have their story and Zahothians need die."

"This is not your decision, Rockha!" I snapped angrily. "That is for the elders to decide. We will set the course back Zahoth and inform them of all that we have discovered. The human, Avi, will be proof of this and the elders will hear her testament whether you like it or not.

"But could we not simply send a communication to the

eld-"

"The Nepharan interference is too strong we would have to get halfway home before we could communicate. Furthermore, the situation requires explanation in person." I interrupted strongly.

Chavak gave me a firm nod of agreement whereas Rockha stayed silent head bowed. "Am I understood, Sergeant?"

He raised his head and looked me straight in the eyes, "yes, Sir, perfectly" he said in a somewhat reluctant manner.

"Good. Chavak you set the course for star XT521."

Chavak went over to the computer and typed in the coordinates. "But, sir, that is in the opposite direction to Zahoth."

"Precisely. Last time we were here, we opened a wormhole so that the supply chain could work more efficiently. It is only a quarter of a light year away from earth and it will take us within spitting distance of Zahoth. Let's just hope it still exists, otherwise it might be too late by the time we get to Zahoth."

"Yes, Sir," Chavak answered optimistically.

"Sergeant Rockha, please go down to inspect the fuel cells and hyper drive. ETD: 15 minutes."

"Yes, Sir," Rockha answered as he turned around swiftly and left the command module. There was something about his behavior that was not sitting right with me. I found myself walking over to the surveillance monitor to make sure that he was doing what I asked. I hated not trusting a member of my crew, but these were exceptional circumstances and we could be in real trouble if I did not have complete control of my men.

Chapter Eight

ROCKHA

WHO DOES that guy think he is? First, he puts us all in this mess with his crazy temper, then he has the audacity to order me around. And Chavak is just a little suck up as well. I never wanted to go on this mission, but the elders wanted 'an experienced engineer.' I've done my time taking orders from the likes of Nevak, they're all the same, claim to be so honorable and honest. But I know that they are exactly like the rest of us. Survival is our greatest instinct, and I will do anything to get out of this shit alive. And following Nevak's orders may mean that I survive this mission, but most likely I will be sent back to this forsaken planet for an actual war. And I have no interest in that. I am only two years of service away from retirement, and I refuse to spend that time locked in an unwinnable battle for a planet I could not give a solitary shit about. I was perfectly happy spending the remainder of my military days on my solitary planet. Living as their god. It was the best gig I could have possibly imagined, and it was taken away from me. I refuse to die for him and iI refuse to die for the life-forms of this planet. They are primitive and stupid. It's their own fault, getting enslaved by the Nepharans, it is not my problem.

I bet this is all to do with that human female. I could sense something in Nevak's voice when he carried her in here. It seemed like genuine concern. The traitorous bastard. Why would he care about her in the slightest? Her own people don't even care about her. I just have this inkling that somehow she has infiltrated the captain's mind. We don't know much about these creatures, maybe they posses some kind of power of which we are ignorant. He must realize that the best thing for Zahoth is to return her to the Nepharans and wash our hands of the entire situation. Killing the Nepharan is bad, but I cannot imagine them starting a war over one life. Especially if they were to get what they wanted out of this meeting.

I have to take matters into my own hands. I am the most experienced soldier on this ship, and sometimes a man has to decide his own destiny. I refuse to let Nevak endanger our planet. I will return the girl myself. Once it's done it's done and we will not have to argue about it any longer. Hopefully, someday, they will both see that what I have done has saved Zahoth from countless heartaches.

I will be unable to enter the captain's quarters, though. I will have to trust in the stupidity of the human to let me in. I don't think Nevak suspects anything, so I should have a couple of minutes to get her out of the ship and once I'm out no one will be able to stop me. I'll take one of our shuttles and leave her at the border of the city in the distance. I'm sure she will be picked up from there. And whatever happens to her, happens.

Chapter Nine

AVI

I WAS FEELING A LITTLE BETTER. Nevak had been gone for about 15 minutes and it had given me some time to accept my situation. I was hoping he would come back soon, so we could discuss what we were going to do about this mess. The last thing I wanted to do was return to my hell-hole of a planet, but, on the other hand, it was the only home I had ever known. Where was I going to go? Planet Zahoth? Even if Nevak would take me, which was a big 'if,' what could I do there. It was a planet of warriors and I was pretty far from a warrior. Anyway - I was getting ahead of myself, I had no idea what Nevak was thinking or even what my options were at this point.

Suddenly, there was a knock on the door. I assumed Nevak would just walk in, so I stayed silent. A second knock folowed by a matter-of-fact statement, "It's Nevak."

I walked over to the door, but had no idea what to do to get it open. "I don't know how to open it," I said while examining around the door for anything that looked like a button. Clearly Nevak had trusted that I would have no idea how to get out of the room due to the confusing array of devices attached to the door. But, more importantly, where would I go?

"Press the touch pad in the right corner with your finger," the somewhat muffled voice said.

I located the touch pad, but I had to jump to reach it. His race was so fucking tall. Not quite the 10 feet we were told, but I'd say at least 8. On my third jump I finally reached it and with a puff the door slid open. I was taken aback as the alien behind the door was revealed to me.

"Who are you?" I asked timidly.

"I'm Rockha. The Captain asked me to bring you to the command module," the alien said with a smile. He was not quite as big as Nevak and he looked pretty different in the face. He had some wrinkles in places which made his face look a little mean and his muscles were not quite as defined. His eyes had a milky quality to them unlike Nevak's which shined brightly. I guessed that he might be a little older.

"Sure, ok," I said and we head down the corridor. We walked down the corridor, him a little ahead of me and he led me to a door right at the far end. He tapped his finger on the touchpad and it opened. We walked in and I realized that we were back in the room we had arrived in. The body of the dead Nepharan and the guards were still there. The sight of them felt less traumatizing since I had learned the truth about my planet, but still a little eerie. I wondered why Rockha had brought me back here. Maybe the command module was adjacent to this place? When Rockha walked over to a large indent in the wall and started typing on a screen, I began to get a little suspicious.

"Where's Nevak?" I asked nervously.

"This is the door to the command module, I'm just opening it. Come closer, don't be shy."

This didn't look like any of the other doors on the ship, but maybe the one to the command module needed special protection. The hexagonal indent began opening slowly, and I saw what looked like the inside of a much smaller space ship and there was no Nevak inside. Suddenly, I started to panic, but before I could run off, Rockha grabbed me by the throat and slammed me to the wall next to the now open entrance.

"I'm taking you back were you belong," he said in his croaky voice. His breath smelled awful, and I flinched at that as much as I was writhing in search for air as his hand crushed my windpipe.

Suddenly a booming noise from the door to the main ship, "Rockha!" it was Nevak, and he was carrying what looked like a sword of some kind, but it was all black and jagged. In his other hand he had the same weapon he shot the guards with and was pointing it at us.

"Let Avi go," he demanded in a firm voice.

"Avi!" Rockha scoffed. "You have been blinded by your unnatural attachment to this... this thing! I am doing what needs to be done. What you don't have the stomach to do."

"We did not agree on this, Rockha, put the human down and we can discuss your concerns."

"It's too late for that. I'm going." With those last words, he threw me into the little ship. I fell on the hard surface and felt a sharp pain in my side. Rockha was just about to come in after me when I heard a shot and he flew to the ground out of my line of sight. Nevak ran into the ship and pulled me out of it and told me to run off. I looked back as I fled and saw Rockha getting up. He had black liquid oozing from a hole in his shoulder and looked fucking pissed off.

"What are you going to do, Captain? Murder one of your men?" he said antagonistically. The warriors now stood only a few feet apart. Nevak was still pointing the gun at Rockha who was now the same shade of red, I had seen nevak as when he killed those men. My heart was racing as I turned around once I got the entrance to the ship to follow what was happening.

"I won't if you don't give me a reason to," Nevak answered calmly.

"I've always known you were too weak to be a commanding officer. I've seen hundreds of kids like you come and go. You're all the same. I provoke the right o khrokkogo."

"Don't be ridiculous, Rockha, I am not going to fight you. Just calm down and come in to talk about this."

"I bet you'll fight if I go for the human," he said as he threw himself rapidly at Nevak. I almost missed it, he moved so fast. The gun flew to the floor and Nevak was down. I saw Rockha charging at me with a malicious grin on his face. I was trying to open the door before he reached me, but he was covering the distance too fast. I was panicking, pressing every pad by the door, but nothing was working. He was only a few feet away from me and I closed my eyes and screamed in horror as he raised his fist. But nothing happened, I opened my eyes and saw Nevak was holding his fist. He had caught up to him and got in between us. He forcefully pulled Rockha's fist to the side and kicked him in the chest. Rockha must have flown like 20 feet and landed with a bang on the hard floor.

"Stay there," Nevak commanded sternly turning his attention back to Rockha. He had now turned that hellish red color and his gaze was focused on Rockha who had recovered from the kick and was once again coming at Nevak. Nevak, in turn, ran towards him and they met in the middle of the hall. Rockha landed a mighty punch in Nevak's face, which probably would have killed any human. I gasped in terror, but Nevak barely reacted. He blocked the next of Rockha's blows and landed one in his abdomen. Rockha stumbled as Nevak continued with a second hit right in his eye. Rockha fell to the ground and as Nevak was about to land his next punch, he sliced Nevak's chest with a blade he had produced from under his kilt. Nevak, who was able to avoid the full force of the swing with an evasive manoeuvre backwards, retreated, allowing Rockha to get up with his blade. I saw Nevak's hand wander to his side, but he noticed, as did I, that his blade lay next to his gun a few yards behind Rockha. Rockha smiled at the sight of Nevak's wound and moved in. Slicing furiously at Nevak. He was able to avoid the first three, but the fourth slice got him in the shoulder and the fifth above the knee. He caught Rockha's hand as he was delivering the knockout blow to the now kneeling Nevak. Nevak looked back at me and seemed to summon strength from nowhere and swept the legs of Rockha from under him with a kick. He fell to the floor with a crash as Nevak released his hand and rushed over to retrieve his weapon. To my astonishment, he left the gun and rushed back over with his blade to the recovering Rockha. Nevak charged towards him and their blades met with a ferocious clang. Nevak looked terrifying. The power and skill with which he wielded his weapon was astonishing. It was like watching two tigers fight to the death, terrifying but exhilarating. The agility with which they were fighting was almost too intense to follow with human eyes. Finally, it looked like Rockha was tiring and Nevak had the upper hand. However, he had not landed a blow yet, and I did not know how he could. Suddenly, I screamed as Rockha wounded Nevak in the ribs with a desperate lunge, Nevak groaned loudly in pain as the black blood sprayed from his side. Rockha pulled his blade over his head in an attempt to end the battle once and for all and brought it down on Nevak. I looked away for a moment expecting the worse but then saw that Nevak had caught the blade in his free hand and in one swift movement plunged his own jagged blade into Rockha's jaw. The other end came out of the top of his head. Rockha stood frozen as his blade fell from his hand and was left in Nevak's. He dropped it and retracted his blade from Rockha's skull and both bodies fell to the floor. One dead, one alive.

I hurried over to the injured Nevak as fast as I could and knelt beside him. His body was covered in nasty cuts, and I could now see that his hand was bleeding profusely from catching Rockha's sword. "Are you ok?" I asked, my voice trembling with concern.

"I'm fine," he said, as he touched stroked my cheek with his thumb.

"I could not let him take you back down there," he said in a soft, quiet voice.

"I know, they would kill me."

"No," he interjected. "That is not the reason why. I could not bare to see you go. Rocka was right, I do care about you. I want to protect you from everything and everyone."

Tears came to my eyes as he stared deeply into them, "I love you, Nevak," I said, voice shaking.

All of a sudden, I could see a change in Nevak's color. He was losing his red and turning a deep purple. He looked at his arms and torso in astonishment. His cuts were healing themselves and slowly vanishing out of sight. "I do not know what this means." He said baffled.

"I have never felt anything like this before. I feel so warm." I noted that his touch on my skin did now feel much hotter.

He looked at me tears filling his eyes and said, "I need you, now."

He grabbed the back of my head, rose up from his position on the floor and kissed me with such intensity I nearly fell backwards. His lips felt amazing. After way too little time, he stopped and seemed like he was waiting for something.

"I do not feel it, Avi. I do not feel the heat rising in me."

I looked at him baffled. Did he mean he wasn't into this? Then I remembered what he had told me about Zahothians and how when they are in heat they become violent. Was he saying that he wasn't feeling that? "How is that possible?" I asked.

"I don't know. I don't know what is happening to me, Avi, but I think you are the one doing it. I feel incredible and warm. Your love is filling me up."

Before I could react, he got up and took me in his arms and began hurriedly carrying me back into the ship.

"Nevak, what are you doing? You're hurt!" I protested

as the alien warrior held me in his strong hands as if I were a tiny bird.

His sole response was, "I need to fuck you, now."

———

We reached Nevak's quarters and I could already feel my pussy getting wet. I could feel his defined muscles as he pulled me towards his tight body. He pressed his finger on the touchpad while holding me up with one arm and the door slid open. He rushed over to the large bed in the center of the room and threw me onto it. He ripped off what was left of my robe, which was basically ruined now, and began hungrily kissing my boobs.

"I am going to worship every inch of you," he said in a soft manly growl.

I moaned in pleasure as his tongue circled my rock-hard nipples. He then graduated to sucking them intensely. He must have been using some weird alien techniques because it felt fucking amazing. I could feel it all the way down in my wet pussy. In moments between the intense feelings of pleasure and excitement, I thought about what an insane day it had been. I had witnessed 4 murders, found out my entire race were slaves to alien overlords, and now I was having sex with an alien warrior who just killed one of his own kind for me.

"I can sense that you are turned on, Avi." He said as he began to lower himself down to my wet slit.

He tore my flimsy panties off in one fell swoop and dove into my cunt.

"The taste and scent is intoxicating," he groaned as he

devoured my pussy with his coarse tongue. I groaned in pleasure even before he found my clit.

"Oh, that's what you like," he said with a smile as he got back to sucking on it.

I was writhing in pleasure and grabbed his smooth head with both hands, pushing him into me. I needed more; I needed him inside me. As I thought this, he began darting his tongue in and out of my greedy hole with amazing speed. I felt like I was being penetrated by a little cock every time his tongue entered me. Suddenly, I felt the point of no return creep up on me while my warrior tongue fucked me. I began screaming with intense delight as my body spasmed uncontrollably in a rough orgasm. Nevak's hands holding my hips in place while he devoured my juices was the only thing stopping me from falling off the bed. As I attempted to catch my breath, Nevak arose from between my legs and untied his kilt. He revealed to me a gargantuan cock, both in length and girth. Unlike the rest of his body, it did not posses that hint of transparency. I could see every large vein as it struggled to reach for the stars. I was able to pull my eyes away from the monster and admire his entire heavenly body. Every particle in him oozed power and strength. His muscles glistened with sweat from his recent battle, and he had a lustful look in his eyes as my naked body was covered with his gaze. I was still lying on the bed, legs wide open ready to give my warrior his prize. He walked over to me and grabbed my hips and turned me over. My face was plunged into the depths of the soft mattress as his strong hand held my ass in place. The most guarded areas of my body were now completely revealed to him, and I felt both ashamed and excited. He gave my naked ass a ferocious slap, and I instinctively arched my back in response.

"This is how we do it on Zahoth," he said in his deep baritone. Even his voice made me wet. I could not wait for his giant cock to enter me. I had obviously fooled around with other underlings at the mine even though it was forbidden, but never had I been taken like this before.

"I want you to tell me that you want my cock, human. Beg for it," Nevak said calmly.

"Please, Nevak, fill my hole, I beg you, fuck me!" I yelled awkwardly. I hoped that didn't sound too ridiculous, but I would say anything at this point to get him to penetrate me.

"In the bedroom, you can call me Master," he said as he slapped my other cheek. I whimpered in a mixture of pleasure and pain. For him the slap was most likely a light one, but I really felt it and I fucking loved it.

"Please, Master, fuck me hard," I begged desperately. I didn't know it was possible to be this desperately horny.

"Very well."

The next thing I felt was my alien master's rock hard shaft plunging into my wet pussy. I gasped in pleasure as it reached the very end of my soft cave, filling me completely. There was something about his cock. Fuck, I think it was vibrating, no; it was more than that. It was like it was surrounded by a field of electricity. Every part of me was tingling with pleasure and nowhere more so than deep inside me. His strong hands grabbed both my ass cheeks, spreading them even wider, exposing me to him even more. He proceeded to fuck me hard but steadily. My dirty blond hair was flying all over the place with the motion and I knew that even if I wanted to stop him, which I fucking didn't, there would be no way I could. He was holding me down with a strength I had never felt. Suddenly, the pumping stopped, and I felt myself lifted off of the bed. He turned me around in midair and pressed me against the wall. Our faces were now touching each other, and he stuck his divine tongue in my mouth at the same time as I felt his cock enter my wetness once again. I bit his lip as he fucked me, and he did not even wince. I clawed at his back, but it did not make a scratch. All I could do was be helplessly pummeled by this his monster cock. He lifted my thighs higher with his defined arms in order to penetrate me even deeper. I gasped into his shoulder as he made me feel things I did not know were possible. I screamed and screamed into his must-scented chest as I exploded in a series of orgasms. I do not even know how many there were, but it felt like the wave lasted a lifetime.

He then threw me back on the bed and said, "one day, I will come inside you and you will carry my baby, but today I will mark you with my seed."

He began furiously wanking his vascular cock as I lay beneath him, completely exhausted and too weak to resist in any way. With a groan, he climaxed hard, his dick convulsing uncontrollably and legs nearly buckling from the force of his orgasm as an unholy amount of cum covered my body. Some of it went in my mouth as I waited to be marked by my master. It tasted amazing, a little like a peach really, much nicer than human spunk. When he finally finished, he collapsed next to me on the bed. He was covered in sweat from the effort and I, feeling completely used, lay there covered in his seed. I was truly his now.

Chapter Ten

NEVAK

As I LAID THERE next to Avi, the whole universe felt tiny. Like everything that mattered was in this room. I had discovered a new side of myself today. I had always been a warrior and a soldier, that was in my blood, but I had never cared for anything quite as I cared for Avi. Of course, I was committed to protecting the universe and all living beings that reside in it, but they were an abstract object, Avi was right here in front of me. Her beautiful long hair, her cute button nose and those light freckles on her cheek. Her curvy vivacious body attached to those slim long legs. She may as well have been a god. That's how perfect she was. And now she was mine. My entire life I felt that I was searching for something to make me truly happy, to give my life real and solid purpose. And here it was and it felt incredible.

It was not just I who had saved Avi; Avi had also saved me. This chemical reaction in my body was not known to me. It was customary for my species to change color according to how we feel, but in my life, I had only ever experienced a handful of emotions, usually the red rage which came out in battle, but never had I felt or even heard of this deep intense purple my body now exhibited. It was not just a change in pigment; the color engulfed my entire being. It was like a bundle of hot energy had accumulated in my chest and the only way to release that energy was to direct it at Avi. When we had merged in love, I could feel the energy expanding into my whole body and mind and finally exploding in release. Even after sex I still felt this energy inside me and it intensified every time I glanced over at that beautiful human. I had to have her again and again, but we had already squandered much time and decisions needed to be made on our future. All that I knew at the moment was that my future would revolve around Avi. She might be the key to everything.

"What you thinking?" Avi asked me as she got out of bed and grabbed a cloth from the storage closet.

"Just about how happy I am, that we found each other," I answered.

"Yeah, me too, but..."

"But what?" I answered quickly, slightly concerned.

"But what are we going to do now? I don't see any other option than to leave, but earth is my home," Avi said solemnly.

"I know, but you have no future here. Listen, I want you to come back to Zahoth with me. I can't explain what is happening, but the elders need to know about this."

"Yeah, what's up with you, I thought you said that you would tear me to pieces if we 'mated,'" the last word left her mouth with a touch of sarcasm.

"I know, and that is always the case and has been for all of history, but you, somehow you are different. There must be some kind of cosmic link between our two species of which we have been unaware. Nothing else can explain this. I believe we are destined to be together, we are destined to be mates. You must come back to my planet with me."

"I don't know, Nevak. What we just did blew my mind, but you have to give a girl a chance to readjust to her situation. I have been through more changes in this single day than I have for the entirety of my life combined. I meant it when I said I love you, but I'm also terrified of leaving my home planet to go to a planet of fierce warriors. What if they don't accept me and what if I don't like it there? There are endless possibilities of failure."

"But we are destined to be together and I will always protect you from any harm."

"But I don't just want to be 'Nevak's human pet,' I want to be my own person. And how can I just leave earth in the hands of these evil monsters?"

"But, Avi there is nothing to be done. I cannot defeat an entire Nepharan army on my own. And I will die before I leave you in their hands. You must come with me."

"I am not yours to order around Nevak!" Avi exclaimed angrily.

"I do not understand why you are getting angry. You feel this as much as I do."

"I just need some time to think, Nevak. You need to give me some time to clear my head. You are coming on very strong. We only just met," she said rather harshly.

I continued to push, "Look at your back, that is how much the humans value you. Why do you care about them at all. Come with me and be happy."

"Earth is my homeɪ Just leave me alone, Nevak!" She screamed.

Her words were like daggers in my heart. I had thought that everything would be great from now on. I could not understand why she felt so attached to a planet and a people that had treated her like a slave her whole life. What was she scared of?

"Ok, I will give you some space," I said sadly while clothing myself once more. I could feel the energy inside me diminishing and my color reverting back to the normal pale blue. I think she noticed this but did not say anything. I left her sitting in the corner with her arms crossed. She looked angry, but I had no idea what I had done wrong. I decided to go fill Chavak in on everything that had happened, he was probably still setting our course. It was a complicated process which needed real concentration. I was not sure how I was going to tell him all that had happened in the past hour.

I touched my finger to the touchpad which opened the sliding door. I took one last look back at Avi sitting in the corner. She did not even look at me as I said, "I love you."

———

I walked down the corridor trying to get my head together. She wasn't the only one to have gone through a lot today. I killed 4 sentient beings, one of which was of my own race. I would be in pieces due to that alone, but, additionally, I had fallen in love, a thing that I did not even think was possible for my species or, at the very least, for me. Chavak was a good man, and I was hoping he would be sympathetic to all that I had to tell him.

I walked into the command module, and Chavak scarcely looked up from his work. Once he noticed it was me, he asked if Rockha had inspected everything necessary for launch. I paused for quite a while, thinking what I should say to him. Finally, I decided on a direct approach, "Rockha is dead, Chavak." I stated sternly, but with a touch of sadness.

"What!?" he answered in surprise. "How?"

I went on to explain to Chavak how he had tried to return Avi to earth despite our decision to the contrary and how he had attacked me head on and I had no choice but to defend myself. Chavak looked completely shocked the entire time I was telling him the grim story.

"But why would he do that, Captain?" he asked in astonishment.

"I don't know, Chavak." I said, putting my hand on his shoulder. " I think he was alone on that planet for too long and had lost sight of what our mission in the universe was. He had become self-centred, much like the humans. And I think this forced him to act out against me. We never got along as you know, even before arriving on earth and the situation here must have been too much for him to handle, but even I never expected him to revoke the right to challenge his Captain. I do not thin there has been a case of that in 50 years, if not more. But one can only speculate at the motivations of another man, all I know is that I was not going to allow him to do what he had planned."

Chavak looked thoughtful for a while and then nodded, "I would have done the same, Captain, he was out of order. I'm just shocked that he would do something like that."

"As am I, but we must move forward. Our situation

has changed. I believe Avi is of great importance, we must get her back to the elders as quickly as possible."

"What is so special about the human, Captain? You said she was in the lower caste of humans. She cannot possibly be of any political significance."

"Not political, Chavak. Biological."

"I don't understand," he answered looking puzzled.

"I don't completely understand myself, but she did something to me. Or, how can I explain this. She made me feel different - she made me feel what the humans call 'love.'"

"What is that?"

"On earth, men and women live together with their young as family units. I am only just beginning to understand how this is possible. I performed the mating ritual with her, Chavak."

"What!?" he shouted in shock. "That is impossible!"

"I know it is. Or, I mean, it should be, but after I saved her from Rockha she said that she loved me and it filled me with this warm energy that emanated throughout my body. Instead of feeling the normal rage of heat I felt the heat, but in the stead of rage I felt, love. It was capable of causing physical changes in me. It healed my body, Chavak. I barely have a mark on me from my battle with Rockha."

"This is remarkable. If what you are saying is true, Captain, and I do not doubt you, then the elders must know. This could have giant implications for our planet. You may have solved the breeding question, we could stop the suffering of our females."

"I know, Chavak, but I am not sure she wants to go with us."

"She has to, Captain! Does she not understand how important this is."

"What can I say, I think something is being lost in translation between the two of us. I think she is still attached to this planet."

"But, if we were to take her and prove to the elders that human females are the missing link, they would be bound to attempt to liberate her people. Everyone would go to war for a cause this great!"

I cannot believe I had not thought of this. If we could show the elders the compatibility between Zahothians and humans, they would have to come to earth's aid. "You're right! I had not thought of that. I must persuade her to join us. Have the ship ready to leave at a moment's notice, Chavak. I will be back shortly."

"Yes, Sir!" Chavak said with a renewed enthusiasm.

I was not sure if I could convince Avi, but, thanks to Chavak, I had now realised that it was not just I who needed Avi; it was my people. I had to convince her to come with me. The fate of my people depended on it.

Chapter Eleven

AVI

I WAS NOT REALLY sure why I was reacting so strongly to all of this. I know Nevak had my best interest at heart, but him telling me that I have to come with him on a journey across the universe was just a little overwhelming. He was being very pushy and bossy, which was a massive turnoff everywhere but in the bedroom. My head knew that I did not really have a choice, but in my heart I knew that I was a human and I belonged here on earth. Maybe there was something I could do to save earth. But that possibility would be gone if I was to leave o this ship. I was just filled with contradicting emotions and thoughts. On one hand, I did really feel love for Nevak. No man had ever treated me with such kindness, and the sex was fucking mind-blowing. But the way he approached our relationship worried me. He could not just tell me what to do and expect me to obey. I wanted an equal partner, someone I could talk to about anything, I was having second thoughts about the whole thing.

I think the reason I cooled on Nevak was precisely the

lack of choice presented to me. At this point, it was basically leave with him or return to earth and probably die. I felt like I was being held at gunpoint by him, which is obviously a completely unfair comparison since he was the one who saved me, twice. But I could not help how I felt. All I wanted was for Nevak to come through that door and tell me that he wants me to come with him and he wants to be with me, not that 'I must go.' I do not like being told what to do by anyone (outside of the bedroom), so although I loved his assertiveness and dominance in some ways, I do not believe that is healthy when it comes to our relationship.

I was looking around for something to wrap myself in, since I was still naked. You would have thought there would be a blanket or something in here, even if it was an alien ship. But I found nothing so, begrudgingly, I resigned myself to wait for Nevak's return. I was not going to go waltzing around the ship in my birthday suit.

I had decided the moment he walked in I was going to hit him with some cold hard facts about the situation and that he can't just order me around if we are to be together. But he barged in with such excitement that I did not have a chance to say anything that I had planned.

"Avi!" He exclaimed as he approached my naked form sitting on the bed. "I know a way to save earth."

This certainly piqued my interest, and I waited for him to elaborate.

"If we can persuade the elders on Zahoth of your race's importance to ours, then they would have to come to earth's aid."

"But why would we be important to you guys? You're

like a race of fearless warriors, aren't you?" I asked, not understanding what he was getting at.

"It seems that females of your race might be compatible for mating with our males. This is something our species has been searching for for thousands of years. Our mating rituals back home are a horrible burden to our females due to the uncontrollable heat rage males get when around a Zahothian woman, but, as you saw your love overcame that. I did not feel any anger or rage as we fucked, all I felt was love."

This concept sounded a little weird to me. How could two completely different species be suited so well for each other? And how would this save earth? I presented these questions to Nevak.

"It's simple. Once we prove to the elders that we are a perfect breeding match, every single warrior on Zahoth will wish to liberate earth from the hands of the Nepharans. There is only one cause that my people would go to war with the Nepaharans for and it is this."

"Ok, I get it, but does this mean you want me to have your baby?" I asked.

"More than anything, Avi, I want to put one in you right now, but we are not yet completely certain whether pregnacy will be possible. Chavak will have to run some tests on you on the way to Zahoth to make sure that you would not be harmed."

"I am willing to accept that there is a possibility what you are saying is all true and we are a perfect match, I certainly feel more for you than I have ever felt for another man, and our sexual connection can't just be a coincidence, but, say we somehow do convince your elders that this is a cause worth fighting for and say you do defeat the Nepharans and liberate earth, what happens then? Will we just be trading one master for another? Are you going to make all human females your baby machines?"

"No, no, of course not. In order for the mating to work there must be a love connection, and this can hardly come about if we were to force your women into mating. It would all be completely voluntary. I assume that your females do find the males of our species somewhat attractive, am I correct?"

I looked Nevak mesmerizing body and chiseled face up and down and said, "yes, I think some women might find you attractive."

"Well, what do you think of the plan then? We head for Zahoth immediately, convince the elders and then we come back to earth to liberate your people from the Nepharan overlords."

"Do you think the elders will be easy to convince?"

"I do not see how they could object, I will have you as living proof."

It was difficult to poke any holes in Nevak's plan, and I was feeling better about the situation. I think what was holding me back was how he had acted moments before. "Nevak, your plan is good, but I feel like you do not understand why I snapped at you before. You cannot boss me around like that, you have to listen to me and really hear what I am saying if this is going to work."

"But, I was just telling you the facts, we are meant to be tog-"

"Again, Nevak, you are not listening to me. I want us to be equal and I do not care what kind of 'fated mates' we are, that desire will never change."

Nevak looked at me thoughtfully and said softly, "I am

sorry, Avi, I did not mean to be so bossy. I have just never felt this way about anyone, and I was afraid I was losing you even before we had begun. I thought being like the warrior captain you fell in love with would get you to change your mind."

"I love that warrior captain, but he has to understand that in this relationship there is no captain, there is only us and we are equal."

Nevak took another long pause and said, "I think I understand, I am sorry. From now on we are equal."

"Good," I said, feeling quite optimistic after getting my point across easily. I think we were just going to have to get used to each other. He was clearly a good listener.

"What about my plan?" Nevak inquired shyly.

"weeeeeeelll -- You've convinced me, but there's just one more thing I need from you," I said with a devilish smile.

"Anything, my love," Nevak answered with that brooding intensity I had grown to love.

"I want you to fuck me again."

The words had barely left my mouth and Nevak had dropped his kilt. How did he get hard so damn fast? He pounced o top of me like the beast he is and entered my pussy.

Chapter Twelve

NEVAK

AVI LOOKED SO beautiful after we had made love. Her eyes glistened with moisture as we stared into each other's eyes after another heavenly session. I had never felt so alive. Something about taking her body and using it exactly how I wanted gave me a huge rush. But knowing that Avi wanted me to do those things to her was even better. I was becoming conscious of the fact that I was not being a very good captain. Chavak was out there planning our course and preparing the ship while I stayed in my quarters fucking our alien guest. I convinced myself that this was research into how our species interacted with one another, but I knew this was no more than an addiction to Avi and her fabulous pussy. All good things must come to an end though, there was much to do before we leave and I needed to get on that immediately. I gave Avi one last kiss, mustering up all the passion I felt inside me and channeling it through my lips. She moaned as our lips touched and this sent me back into the throngs of lust, but I was able to let go of her as I promised myself once we were on our way we would not be disturbed by anything.

As I got up and put on my uniform, admiring Avi's naked form one last time, she demanded I bring her something to wear.

"I think we have a female uniform in the supply room, it might be a little big for you though..." I said.

"Better than nothing, though," she answered playfully.

I dropped by the supply room and picked out the smallest size we had. I returned to my quarters and handed it to Avi. I grabbed her ass and pulled her close, giving her a final kiss. "Come out when you're ready," I said as I exited the room.

I walked over to the command module to make sure everything was running smoothly. Chavak informed me that everything was ready for take-off, except for the checks Rockha was supposed to run, and he had seen no signs of humans or Nepharans anywhere within a 5-mile radius. It looked like they had not noticed anything yet, or they had and did not care. Either way, we were out of here. I told him to take a break and I would go perform the checks.

I was no trained engineer, but as far as I could tell, we were ready for takeoff. The fuel cells were now at maximum capacity after I initiated the refill and there were no signs of disrepair anywhere in the hyper-drive. I returned to the command module and discovered that Avi had joined Chavak there. Avi looked magnificent. She had somehow made the female top fit her perfectly and you could see the entirety of her long, sexy leg through the skirt which she had folded so that it was not dragging on the floor. She looked like a warrior, a sexy one. They seemed to be engaged in a pleasant discussion.

"I'm afraid I could not tell you too much about the human female anatomy, I'm sorry, I'm no expert," Avi said with a laugh.

"Stop grilling the human, Chavak," I said playfully.

"I'm not grilling her, Captain, but, as a doctor, I am extremely interested to discover what it is the makes these beings so compatible with us. Would it be alright if we conducted some tests to make sure that you are correct, Captain?" he asked, clearly bubbling with excitement.

Before I could answer, he turned to Avi and continued, "with your permission, of course. I promise they won't hurt a bit"

Avi and I looked at each other and smiled. I had realized that Avi did not appreciate my domineering attitude anywhere other than in private, so I did not answer at all but simply nodded towards her encouragingly.

"That would be fine, I guess," she answered, looking a little nervous.

"Marvelous!" Chavak exclaimed. "Once we head off, I will prepare the lab. Speaking of heading off, was everything in order, Captain"

"Yes, Chavak, we will depart in 10 minutes, set the course and prepare the hyper-drive."

"Yes, Sir," he said excitedly.

He went to work, and I went over and placed my hands on Avi's shoulders. She looked good sitting in the captain's chair. She turned her head up at me and asked, "is there anything I should know about space travel before we leave?"

"No, not really. Our ships are very advanced, you probably will not even notice it. Although, going through the wormhole may feel a little weird, but we will not be there for a while."

She grasped my hand and held it to her heart. This felt so right. Chavak returned and said we were ready to go. Avi and I switched places, me taking my seat in the captain's seat. She placed her arms around me ad nuzzled my neck with her soft lips and went to take her seat at Rockha's old place. Chavak took his seat at the front of the module. He would be the pilot. I started the atmosphere engines one by one until all four were running smoothly. The ship rose off the ground with as we engaged the camouflage setting. Did not want any curious humans, or worse, Nepharans reporting a UFO. We slowly hovered above lad before Chavak guided us into a steady ascent. As we flew higher and higher I turned over to look at Avi. I saw that she was crying as she stared out of the window. I unbuckled myself from my seat and walked over and wrapped my arms around her.

"We'll be back soon, my love, and once we're done, you might eve be able to call this place home again."

She looked up at me with her tear-filled gaze and squeezed my arms. "Captain, you better take your seat, initiating hyper drive in 10 seconds."

I gave Avi a kiss on the cheek and walked back over to my seat. The earth just looked like an atmospheric fish bowl now as we exited its atmosphere.

"3, 2, 1, initiating." Chavak said.

We felt a strong jolt of acceleration before the ship's gravity equalizer kicked in and the thrust became peaceful stagnation. We were traveling at a force of over 50 g's, without the equalizer we would all collapse into ourselves under the pressure.

"All systems look good, Captain."

"Good work, Chavak. Relieved."

The ship would now travel automatically to the programmed coordinates. We should be at the wormhole in a few days.

"Permission to begin the tests on the huma... Avi, Sir?"

I looked over at Avi, who was looking a little better, although I could still see the remnants of tears on her red cheeks. She gave me a smile and a quick nod.

"Granted, I will join you."

Chapter Thirteen

AVI

CHAVAK WAS the third of Nevak's species that I had met and it was becoming apparent that even in a race of intergalactic warriors there was a big difference in personalities among the men. He was a little smaller than Nevak but he was still very well defined. He had no tattoos and his face was softer and more rounded than Nevak's. He did have this boyish charm about him, and I was not surprised to find out that he was a little younger than Nevak. He was very excited to show me all his equipment and was clearly very interested in me, or at least my body. If it wasn't for Nevak's presence, I would have been really scared among all the strange equipment. I could, quite literally, not recognize a single one of their devices.

"Holy fuck!" I exclaimed loudly as I was confronted by a massive alien corpse floating in some kind of chamber. It looked like something out of a horrific nightmare.

Nevak laughed and said, "it's ok, that is just Qroko. He is a good friend of mine and really a very pleasant man. Unfortunately, we had some trouble with his cryogenic stasis chamber. He will be fine once we get back to Zahoth.

Recovering from my coronary, I fumbled over to the examination table and Chavak went to work, trying to suppress his grin. He placed some small silicone tabs all over my body. Before he did so he rubbed them with a kind of transparent gel. I must have had about 20 of them on me now. The gel was kind of tingly; it felt almost nice. Like an electric massage. Nevak was over by their equipment with Chavak. They were both very interested in all the monitors. As I lay there on the cold table, I thought about what was to come. I was going to be the first human to see an alien planet. I know my thoughts should have been on this unimaginable world, but all I could think about was earth. Everyone I had ever known was on that watery planet. Every experience, every moment was confined into its atmosphere, but here I was headed for a planet in a different galaxy. In human terms, it may as well be in another dimension. And in a few weeks' time I would be in front of the elders pleading for them to save my planet. If it was not for the love I felt for Nevak, I would have felt desperately lonely. The final hope of humanity. I just hoped there would be something left when I returned.

My melancholy thoughts were cut short by Chavak walking over to me and said that he was experiencing some kind of electromagnetic interference in the equipment. With horror, I remembered the tracking chip the Nepharan had placed inside me. What if they were able to hear everything that had happened since then? Having heard my confession, Chavak rushed over to retrieve a small black gun-like device. I tensed up a little as he placed it on the spot I had pointed out. He pulled the trigger, and the chip flew out of my body. I barely felt a pinch. He placed it in his computer and began laughing.

"It is not even a tracking chip, he said. It has absolutely no data. All it does is omit a tiny electromagnetic field."

Of course, they did not even care about me enough to actually track me. Classic.

Chavak threw the chip out and continued his examination of my body. It was not long until he was exclaiming in excitement, "this is amazing! Her biology is a perfect match for Zahothian males."

"Yes, I told you that I was able to perform the ritual, Chavak." Nevak answered.

"No, you do not understand, Captain. She is not just perfect from a sexual perspective. It's almost as if her body was designed to bare our children. For some reason there has been a mutation in our own females making it dangerous for them to reproduce. It has gotten better over the years due to societal pressure on them for hundreds of thousands of years, but it will still be millions before they can reach the dimensions that Avi has. Her womb is an ideal size and her hips are much wider than a Zahothians allowing for a much safer birth. I see no reason why our two species could not mate. " Chavak explained in a heated excitement.

Before either of us could get a word in, he continued, "the probability of biological characteristics this optimal appearing on a planet more than a hundred light years away is so minuscule it could probably not even be presented in a mathematical formula. It is almost as if this was fate. However, I am unable to explain the other effects

she has on you though. That will require further research,"
Chavak said somewhat disapointedly.

"That's ok, Chavak, great work." Nevak said encouragingly..

I felt a little weird hearing an alien talk about my body
in such a scientific way. It was like I was a rare animal, but
if this meant that I could be with Nevak then I didn't care
what I had to endure. Nevak walked over and ran his
fingers through my hair, lightly brushing my forehead with
his electric touch. Chavak also walked over and began
removing the little thingies from my body.

Once I was cleaned up, we all went to what I assumed
was their version of a kitchen. Something I had not
thought of was what I was going to eat for the duration of
the journey. Luckily, Chavak was ahead of me and assured
me that their food was completely compatible with my
biology and that they had also originated from a planet
whose life forms were based on dihydrogen monoxide, or I
other words: water. It really was remarkable how similar
we were, but at the same time so different. If one of these
guys walked up to you on the street, you would crap your
pants, but after a little while you started to get used to
them and I saw them as almost human. Super strong
warrior humans, but still. Their ration packs weren't that
bad. They had kind of a citrusy taste to them with a bread-
like consistency. I had lived off gruel for my whole life, so,
in a sense, this was a step up.

As we ate our rations, Nevak explained the theory of
relativity to me. They did not call it that, but I did
remember something about that guy with the big white
hair in basic training. They had not told us much about
it. Only that the Nepharans and Zahothians had under-

stood it well and were able to travel the universe on its foundation. He said that although the trip would only take a couple of weeks for us. A couple of years would have passed o earth by the time we had reached Zahoth. Chavak explained that going through a wormhole was an abstract business and they could never calculate the time difference exactly, but based on earlier travel he estimated that it would be 1.7 to 2.3 earth years until we reached Zahoth. Coming back would be approximately the same. It was difficult for me to wrap my head around the fact that I would be barely aging while the earth would continue turning hundreds of times in my absence. I thought of all the people down there stuck in the mines and how long they would have to suffer before we could help them. Nevak explained that for centuries they had operated on a universal sense of time. They no longer talked about years at all since almost all of their inhabitants at one point or another had entered a wormhole or gone into cryogenic stasis. Although a Zahothian natural lifespan was only marginally different to that of a human's (about 120 years on average), Nevak had been born almost 300 earth years ago but was only 38 years old.

All of this sounded bonkers, but it was difficult not to believe it while sitting on an alien spacecraft about to enter a wormhole. It only took us the day to reach the entry to the hole and as we prepared to enter, I immediately regretted asking Chavak for an explanation of what exactly a wormhole is.

"Well, wormholes are actually not that complicated at all. They are consistent with the general theory of relativity. It is a structure amassing a large amount of electromagnetic energy linking disparate points of space and time."

"Maybe I need some kind of example," I said, attempting to mask my confusion.

Chavak turned his head around, looking for an object until he settled on the small rubber place mat right under his gaze. He picked it up and continued his explanation, "you see this sheet. Imagine that is is space. Although obviously space has many more dimensions than a simple object, but for example's sake imagine this."

I nodded as he folded the mat in two, "what a wormhole does is create a link from one point in space to another."

He took a small knife from his belt and plunged it through the rubbery surface, puncturing both sides so that the knife's point came out the bottom.

"Now imagine we travel along this blade from one point in space to another. We are able to circumvent the log distance needed to get from point A to point B due to the bending of spacetime."

I was able to grasp this idea and stopped myself from asking about the time dilation to avoid something way too complicated for my unscientific brain.

We took our seats in the command module as we approached the wormhole. From the spacecraft window I could see a vast bend. It did not really look like a hole it was more like a pitch black waterfall leading into darkness. Nevak strapped me into a seat and gave me a kiss, "do not worry, this is completely safe," he said sensing my nervousness. Unfortunately, his assurances did not put me much at ease as I looked into the pixilated darkness.

"One minute to entry, Captain."

Chavak said from the front seat. Nevak took his seat in the captain's chair and fastened himself in.

"20 seconds."

I could suddenly sense a sharp acceleration, as if we were being pulled in by a massive force.

"5 seconds."

I felt a strong sense of pressure on the front of my body as the g-forces hit me. The side of my face became pressed against the seat as I was unable to hold it in place any longer due to the overwhelming force thrusted upon me. Out of the window I saw a sea of stars in the distance which all at once were engulfed by darkness as Chavak announced, "entering wormhole."

It is difficult to describe exactly what I experienced while going through the black hole. Time and space lost all meaning for me. It was, in a sense, a dream-like state. Everything I once knew felt like a trifle, the only thing that mattered was the present which, in itself was difficult to grasp. Each moment would go by before I was conscious of it. All I could see were flashes of color and different unbelievable scenes, which may have been hallucinations, but there was no way of knowing what they were. i felt at one with the universe, I no longer had a body and was able to travel the universe with my mind. Once on the other side, I felt both that I had experienced an entire lifetime, as well as a sense that the whole experience had lasted less than a split second. i whole-heartedly wished to return to that state of bliss which I had experienced, real life now felt mundane and obsolete. I had this overwhelming sense of anxiety deep inside me for no apparent reason. Slowly, however, I was pulled out of my trance by the reality I had been experiencing for my entire life. I saw Nevak's face and was brought back into me.

"Are you ok, Avi?" I heard his deep voice boom as my senses readjusted to reality. I felt his hand on my thigh and inhaled his scent as his form entered my line of vision.

"Yes," I answered softly as I was overwhelmed with a sense of joy. I was Avi, and he was Nevak and this is where I belonged. He was my past, present and future. The warmth I was felling in my chest exploded as a kiss onto Nevak's unexpecting lips. He returned my enthusiasm, and we embraced in a beautiful passion. I finally pulled away and looked into his eyes, and all my doubts about leaving earth flew away.

"Captain, all systems are operational and looks like we have only lost year months and approximately 270 days."

Never paused for a few seconds before he answered, seemingly not wanting to break the connection between us.

"Excellent news, Chavak, estimated time of arrival on Zahoth?"

"4 days, Captain."

"Set the course and consider yourself relieved for the time being."

"Yes, Sir."

"And, splendid work, Chavak."

"Thank you, Sir." He answered with a smile.

Chavak went to work as Nevak turned his attention to me.

"I think we better make sure you are ok. The first wormhole trip can often be quite shaking. Why don't you join me in my quarters?" Nevak said, pretending to be formal. I think my sense of humor was beginning to rub off on him.

He took me by the hand and led me to his quarters and the door had barely closed when he grabbed my waist with both hands and pulled me close to him for another dream-like kiss.

Chapter Fourteen

NEVAK

THE LAST FEW days have been the best in my entire life. I am unable to keep my hands off Avi. The way she looks, moves, smells... it is like I have an insatiable thirst that cannot be quenched. Fortunately, there had been very little that needed to be done during our voyage to Zahoth and I could therefore devote all my attention to this divine creature. The feeling of love inside me had only strengthened, and every time I saw Chavak he had commented on a change in my complexion. I felt like she was changing me in the deepest parts of my soul.

However, there was one thing gnawing at me. I had made our plan sound simple to Avi as I had not wanted to worry her, but, in all actuality, it was going to take a lot of work to convince the elders of what I was going to tell them. It was also likely that upon arrival I will be arrested. If by some miracle they have not found out about the killing of the Nepahran and the earthlings, then when they find Rockha's body, which will be immediately, I will be taken in for interrogation. Zahoth looks upon the killing of another Zahothian as the worst crime imaginable. There are few reasons to ever do so, and unless I can convince them of the importance of Avi, my reasons will be insufficient and I will be sentenced to death. I had been able to block all of this out of my mind in order to enjoy my time with Avi, but now that I could see my planet and we had begun our descent into its atmosphere, I was forced to face this reality once again.

It was early and as I stared at Avi's naked, sleeping form, I was filled with a sense of fear I had never felt before. I guess it takes having something to lose to be afraid. I was not afraid for myself, but afraid for her. If I do not succeed in my mission, then what will become of her? Failure was not an option.

I could not bring myself to disturb Avi when I got up to go supervise our landing. Chavak was already diligently at the controls as the last part of our journey required a pilot. We greeted each other warmly as we had done each morning and sat down in our respective seats. I had also promised myself I would allow no harm to come to Chavak. He had proven himself as an excellent soldier and a great friend. The responsibility for this mission would be mine and mine alone. I know that he will try to help me anyway he can, but ultimately our fate is in my hands.

We received clearance from ship control and touched down on Zahoth. I had not been back for over a year. It felt good to be home, but I could feel my heart racing as we docked. Chavak knew the situation as well as I did and he gave me a worried glance as control of the ship was taken by mission control. We were pulled forward through the underground tunnel into the main docking area located inside one of our numerous mountains. This was

one of multiple bases on Zahoth and each base could
house thousands of ships. Mission control guided us into
an empty space, and finally we touched down. I could see
that we were being expected. The ship was surrounded by
more than a dozen soldiers and before we could begin our
disembarking procedure, the doors were opened from the
outside and the ship was stormed by the troopers. I knew
there was nothing I could do now, I just had to wait for my
time to speak. I began to think that maybe I had made a
mistake keeping Avi in the dark, this would surely come as
more of a shock to her, in the end, but there was nothing I
could do about that now, besides, I could not bring myself
to ruin what could possibly be our last time together.

Neither I nor Chavak attempted to resist as we were
taken from the ship.

Chapter Fifteen

AVI

I HAD BEEN TREATED WELL by the Zahothians during my incarceration. It seemed to me that I was being held mostly for my own safety. I had not seen much of the planet but on my way from and to my quite comfortable cell I could see glimpses of the outside world. The terrain was black and harsh. Scolded concrete mountains as far as the eyes could see littered with the odd white ash tree here or there. Nevak had told me that their planet was barren, but I was still surprised to see how true that was. Chavak had been to see me multiple times during the past few days. He had told me that Nevak was being tried for treason and murder, but had exonerated everyone else on board with his testimony. Chavak had tried to speak up for him, but Nevak would not allow it. It sounded like my man alright, stubborn as ever. Chavak assured me that everything was going to be ok, but I had a horrible feeling in my gut that he was lying to me. The nerves were making it impossible for me to eat and I think the Zahothian guards were starting to think that I did not even have to, which was fine by me, for the time being. Chavak explained that Nevak had barely had a chance to defend himself yet as it took time for the elders to convene in a single location, and a trial of this magnitude required all of them. Murder was almost unheard of on Zahoth and therefore not taken lightly.

In addition to my nervousness, I was furious at Nevak. Once again he had to go on with his macho bullshit and leave me in the dark. I love how protective he is, but I'm not a child. However, I had moments where I knew that he was doing what he thought was best for me and for us, which then quickly turned back into rage again. It is very difficult trying to hate someone who was basically willing to sacrifice themselves for you. No matter how stupidly he went about it, I still loved him more than anything and these days apart from him just alone with my thoughts had been the most torturous of my entire life.

I was happy to be summoned into the visitation area once again, for at least during my talks with Chavak I was not alone with my morbid thoughts. I felt my heart drop into my stomach as I noticed, to my surprise, this time, I was not greeted by Chavak but, instead, a Zahothian I had never seen before. Did this mean that Chavak had been arrested too? I eyed the visitor up and down. He was even bigger than Nevak and kind of looked like him apart from the long thin ponytail running down from his head. There was something familiar about him, but I could not quite put my finger on it. But then it hit me. He was the guy from the tank on the ship! I knew I recognized him. Nevak told me his name, but I could no longer remember.

"Greetings, Avi, my name is Qroko." the alien said standing up as I sat down across from him.

"Hi," I answered timidly.

"Where is Chavak?" I continued with a small shake in my voice.

"Do not worry, he is fine. He is getting prepared to testify on Nevak's behalf as we speak."

My eyes widened in surprise, "does this mean that the trial is starting?"

"Yes, the elders have convened and the trial will begin at first moon."

This information felt like relief, but it was the kind of relief you experience after dreading a dentist's appointment and he finally opens the door into his office. You are still dreading the procedure, but at least you are finally there.

"I have come to ask you for a favor," Qroko gave a loud sigh and continued, "this is rather awkward, but since I was cleared from hospital after the blunder with my cryogenic stasis, Chavak has filled me in on the situation and I think it is likely Nevak will be sentenced to death."

At these words, I covered my mouth to stop myself from screaming and could feel my eyes welling up.

"I'm sorry, Avi, I did not mean to upset you. I meant to say that I think in the current state of affairs it is likely the elders will see him as a murderer, even with Chavak's testimony there is no way that the council will accept saving your life as a justified reason to take the life of a Zahothian. This is - unless..." Nevak paused once again and looked somewhat bashful, it seemed difficult for him to keep eye contact with me.

"Unless, you complete the mating ritual with him," he said finally.

I think he could see the surprise in my eyes, because he continued immediately, "I realize that this is not a custom on your planet and I would never ask you to do this unless the life of my best friend hung in the balance. I have not seen Nevak since he met you, but Chavak swears that there is something about you, about your species that affects us in a special way. I have no reason to doubt what he says, since I can see he is as determined to save Nevak as I am."

Nevak had not told me too much about the mating ritual, except that it was often fatal to their women. The other detail that stuck in my mind was that it was a public spectacle. I now understood why Qroko had been so shy; I think he was asking me to have sex in front of a crowd of people.

"If what Chavak, has told me is correct, you should be in no dang-"

"I'll do it," I interrupted. There was no question in my mind. If this is what it took to save Nevak then it had to be done.

Qroko seemed relieved. And in a quiet tone said, "I am starting to see why Nevak has taken such a shine to you. It is clear to me that there is some connection between our species. I can feel it when I look at you. Nevak and I have been through a lot together and I thank you deeply for the sacrifice you are going to make. I am honored to have met you, Avi." He reached out his massive hand, and I reciprocated. I could feel Nevak in his touch and this made me sad. I missed him so much.

"You're a good friend, Qroko, I cannot wait to get to know you better once we have saved Nevak."

"I feel the same, Avi. Now, I have arranged for our transport to the elder's hall. Unfortunately, I was not able to gain permission to extract you until the last minute, so we must hurry to make it to the trial on time."

We released our grip simultaneously and rushed out of the room.

Chapter Sixteen

NEVAK

"Nevak Drokhoggo, you stand accused of murder and treason, how do you plead?"

"Not guilty, honored elders."

I heard a murmur in the crowd as these words left my lips. In front of me was the council of elders consisting of the original 7 members. The elders lived in a constant state of hibernation unless called on to adjudicate or rule. All of them were over 1000 years old. They had accumulated their vast knowledge in their lifetime until the age of approximately 80 years, when they were inducted into the council. They were wise beyond reason, and their judgment was final. My case had created quite a stir on Zahoth. It turned out that the Nepharan's were much quicker to react than we had thought. It did not take them long to realise what had happened aboard my ship, and they promptly deduced that this was presumably the act of a rogue soldier. Therefore, they had immediately sent word to the leaders of Zahoth that they had a traitor in their midst. How they were able to relay this message so fast was a mystery to me, but it had, nonetheless, reached Zahoth 2 days before our arrival. For this reason, we had been greeted by the planetary guard as soon as we docked.

Upon searching the ship they found the body of the Nepharan, the two human guards and to the dismay of the search party the body of a fellow Zahothian, Rockha. Considering the circumstances, I considered myself quite lucky. If we had been in a battle zone, I would most likely have been executed on the spot. Murder is such a rare occurrence in our society that any case is handled swiftly and severely. Although I stood humiliated in front of the elders and the large crowd present at the trial, my thoughts were only for Avi. I knew my people, and I trusted that she was being treated well, so there was no worry there, but I worried for her state of mind. I had taken her away from her home dozens of galaxies away, to become a prisoner on an alien planet. Doubtless, she was scared and alone at this very moment, and that thought tortured me more than anything.

Arkoth Braggo, the chairman of the council, silenced the murmuring crowd with his loud booming voice and proceeded to address me, "you may state your case, Captain Drokhoggo."

I took two steps forward and bowed my head in thought. I realized that there was no use sugar-coating anything; I had done what I had done and I would have to tell the truth. I took a deep breath and began my statement:

"Honored Council and people of Zahoth. I stand accused of murder and treason. Two of the most heinous crimes known in our society. I am aware that the nature of these accusations already makes some of you see me differently, but I implore you to listen to what I have to say."

I paused for a moment to make sure I had the attention of everyone in the great hall. Apart from a few murmurs in the crowd I heard total silence and, therefore, continued my speech:

"I am innocent of both charges presented against me. Yes, I did kill Rockha Drakho."

The crowd arrested in a roar of disapproval at these words, and it took the intervention of Arkoth Braggo to calm the crowd down, "Silence! We live in a just and equal society, and these values are extended to its every member. Captain Drokhoggo will be permitted to deliver his entire statement without interruption, and then, but only then, will we pass judgment upon him." The councilmen nodded towards me in a gesture to proceed, I returned the gesture and once again proceeded:

"I did kill the sergeant, however, there is something that you do not know. I killed him for love. I recognize that this word means nothing to most of you and I myself am only just beginning to understand it, but everything I did -- I did for Zahoth."

"Please elaborate, Captain, I am not sure I understand. How was murdering a Zahothian good for Zahoth?" Asked the head councilman.

"Sergeant Rockha was attempting to hand the human over to the Nepharans. He was out of his mind and would not listen to reason. I only acted in self-defense.'"

"But why would you put the life of this human over the life of your crew member, Captain?" The councilman inquired gravely.

"The Nepharans have enslaved the humans' planet. I

have learned of the atrocities conducted by them on this planet, and I was not prepared to throw an innocent back into their grasp. They were willing to give her as a sacrifice to us, the least I could do was not return the favor."

"We understand better than anyone, the length the Nepharans will go to keep their society alive, Captain, however, you disobeyed a direct order when you killed their ambassador, not to mention the humans, and on top of all this you have admitted to killing one of our own. This was supposed to be a simple and peaceful mission. You must appreciate that these happenings require a very good explanation."

I stared at the councilman and realized I had no choice, but to try and explain what had happened to me, "there is something about humans that is -- difficult to explain. I mated with the human female we had on board and I felt completely different, I did not feel anger or rage, I only felt what they call love. I cannot explain this feeling it is some kind of higher power that we have no word for. Somehow our species, which are separated by hundreds of light years are connected in some way. I believe I was meant to find Avi and I believe we are meant to be together and I would do anything to protect her and our bond."

"Are you the only one to have felt this 'connection,' Captain?"

"Yes," I answered solemnly.

"And you are saying that you were capable of mating with this human without endangering her?"

"Yes."

The crowd burst into murmurs once more, I heard especially the females' voices this time.

"You realize how difficult this is to believe, do you not, Captain?"

"Yes, Councilman, I do, but that is why I did what I did. I believe that the humans may be our saviors, but first, we must save them."

"I am afraid, Captain, that without proof, this is very difficult to believe. We have read the statement of your Sergeant, but find his claims of a shared anatomy with the humans unconvincing. It is the belief of this council that you have influenced Sergeant Chavak in some way. For this reason we are not allowing him to testify at this trial and as there are no further witnesses to these crimes, we must conclude-"

The councilman was interrupted by a loud boom at the back of the hall. I turned around, startled to find Qroko and Avi in the entrance. I was so shocked I could not move. I just stared at both of them. I had thought I was never going to see my beloved again and there she stood, looking as beautiful as ever. The crowd parted, and they walked up to me. The guards were so startled by the presence of a human that they stood as still as I did.

Bracken walked up close to me and whispered, "ask permission to perform the ritual."

My eyes widened in shock as my attention transferred to Avi. She gave me one of her cute smiles and a slight nod of approval. They had clearly discussed this beforehand.

"I cannot do that to Avi," I answered abruptly.

Avi clasped my hand in her's and said, "it's ok, I want to do it."

I looked deep into her eyes and said, "you understand what this means? It means we will have to make love in from of everyone."

"I know, and I'm fine with it. It's a small price to pay to Dave your life, Nevak."

I mouthed the words 'thank you' to her and released her from my grasp for hopefully the last time. I could feel that burning feeling of desire and love heating up in me once more. Just laying eyes on her was enough to set it off. During this time the councilmen had been waiting patiently for our deliberation to end, I could feel their gazes on me, and it was not just there's the whole crowd saw the change happening in me and everyone stood in absolute silence awaiting what we had to say.

"I wish to perform the ritual with the human Avi," I declared in my mightiest voice.

Chapter Seventeen

AVI

IT DID NOT TAKE LONG for the council to be persuaded to observe the ritual. If they were to give Nevak a fair trial, it would have to be done. There was nothing more to be said. His entire defence rested on the fact that we were in love. I do not think any of the Zahothians had any idea what that meant, but I guess they were about to find out. Nevak explained on the way that they had a few arena-type constructions built for the performing of the ritual and that, generally, no one mated in any other way due to how dangerous it was. The whole mass that was present at the trial was eager to see the continuation of the trial, and as we flew through the city in the elders' spacecraft, it seemed that even more people were joining in. It was like a snowball cascading through the alien city. Nevak had not released my hand the entire time. And I was beginning to feel the nerves as well. Were we really going to fuck in front of everyone? The thought was so far from reality for the entirety of my life, I do not think that the concept had ever even crossed my mind.

Once we arrived in the circular dome which looked much like the building we just left, we were both stripped naked and left on our own by a large solid black gate. We stood there hand in hand and could hear the crowd murmuring right outside. We both looked at each other, hearts racing, and squeezed our hands together, hard.

"We can still back out, Avi, you don't have to do this." Nevak said gently.

I looked straight up at him and said, "we're doing this whether you like it or not."

We both smiled and turned our heads back to the door. Slowly it creeped open, revealing a blinding light. My eyes strained as they attempted to adjust to the change. I saw an audience of at least a thousand people, probably more. I could see the council members straight ahead in what, presumably, was the alien version of a V.I.P. area. In the middle of the oval arena there was a rather large mattress type thing that actually looked a little more like a wrestling mat. Nevak took the lead and guided me forward as I stared every which way, trying to take in the scene. We came to the centre of the mat which had suddenly become surrounded by guards, but Nevak instructed them to stand back claiming that they would not be needed. The guards looked at each other perplexed, but ultimately took a few paces back, giving us some breathing space. Nevak bowed to the council members and then turned to me. I did not understand how he was acting so calm, I was already sweating bullets and I could feel my heart pounding in my chest. He took my face into his hands gently and looked deep into my eyes. This had an immediate calming effect on me and I almost forgot we were standing naked in front of a massive crowd. The fact that the crowd was completely silent almost made the experience more eerie. There was a sense of anticipation in the place.

He pulled himself close and lowered his forehead onto mine and said, "it's just you and me, Avi."

His strength was infectious. I felt that I could do anything with him holding me like this.

"We will just show them how much we love each other and then no one will come between us ever again," He continued in his softest voice.

I nodded slowly and still staring into each other's eyes, we fell gently on to the mat and Nevak kissed me with that burning intensity to which I had now become so accustomed. I could feel his massive cock growing against my leg as we continued to make out. He broke our kiss and climbed on top of me, guiding his cock to the entrance of my hole.

We continued focus only on each other and simultaneously we both said, "I love you."

He pushed himself deep inside me and I whimpered in pleasure, grabbing onto his muscular back to brace myself. We continued to stare into each other's eyes, his beautiful deep black eyes, as he slowly began pumping me with his pleasure-giving shaft. I once again felt that miraculous tingle throughout my entire body as he slowly picked up the pace. I could feel that my pussy was already sopping wet as he lovingly kissed my neck. On the ship we had fucked alright, but I felt this was the first time we were making love. He was being so tender and careful; it made me feel like a fragile treasure. After a while I started to get tired of this vanilla shit and something clicked in my mind, where I was like *fuck it, if they want a show let's give them a show.*

Somehow, the adrenaline gave me the strength to push Nevak onto his back, I could see the surprise in his eyes as I hurried to straddle him. I don't think I had ever been on top before. I plunged his moist cock deep into my wet cunt and fiercely slammed my hands on his strong chest. This time I looked around to see the gasping faces of the crowd as I, a human, fucked one of these warriors. Suddenly, the thousands of gazes on me became a massive turn on. Everyone could see my perky tits bouncing up and down as Nevak's veiny, electric dick went in and out of me. I looked the head councilman straight in the face as my ass slabbed against Nevak's thighs faster and faster. His hands grabbed my ass cheeks pulling me down faster and faster, I could feel his penis beginning to spasm in the unmistakable signs of orgasm. This would be the first time he had ever come inside me, and I could not wait to feel his seed fill me up. The thought of it brought me to the brink of orgasm as I looked around, taking pleasure in the shocked stares from the crowd. Nevak began to groan that manly groan as I felt his cock explode into me and I screamed in ecstasy as I felt the waterfall of liquid gush deep inside wave after wave in sync with the waves of my massive climax.

I collapsed on top of my man enjoying the last sensation of his dick leaving my now satisfied pussy. We laid there for what felt like an eternity of bliss, before the arena erupted in thunderous applause and elated screams.

EPILOGUE

1 month later

Avi

THE LAST MONTH had been quite hectic. Ever since our 'performance' at the arena, we have become celebrities on planet Zahoth. I have been greeted in the street with cheers every time I have gone out. Especially the women of Zahoth would approach me and offer their gratitude. It was all a little overwhelming, but it was nice to be appreciated for once in my life, even if it was for my compatible genitalia. Luckily the atmosphere on Zahoth is quite agreeable. After the initial shock of the light gravity, I feel I have no become fully accustomed to life here. This is especially aided by the almost magical technology available to the Zahothians. The entire settlement is covered in a large atmospheric bubble, which keeps the temperature at a reasonable 40 degrees Fahrenheit. The Zahothians like it cold. I have not seen much of the planet due to the harsh conditions outside of the settlement, but Nevak has promised me a trip before we leave.

Speaking of Nevak, he has been the perfect man. He is spending a lot of his time on science and military committees as a consultant, but every moment he is at home is bliss. We have a sizable apartment in the centre of town. I have been told that first apartments are generally not quite as nice as ours, but because of our special status it was agreed that I should be out and about as much as possible to spread the word of the 'miracle.' That's right, I was now pregnant with Nevak's child. As I am the first (known) human to be impregnated by a Zahothian and Nevak is the first Zahothian to impregnate and alien, I have been under scrupulous medical surveillance. I have been told that it is likely I will give birth to a healthy baby boy within a month. Which is lucky, because even after only a month, I am massive.

After the mating ritual, the Zahothian elders sprung into action and Nevak was able to convince them that an operation to free earth from the Nepharans was both beneficial and necessary. Due to the fact that mine and Nevak's biological compatibility was now a matter of public record. Everyone supported the mission. All the veterans of the earth war were being called up, and the planet was preparing for a full-on invasion of earth.

It was a very exciting time in many ways, but we still found time to enjoy the little things. Nevak had become much more caring since I became pregnant and lost some of that possessiveness he exhibited in the beginning stages of our love. As I sat at our kitchen table pondering the amazing journey of the last few months, sipping on a popular drink that was remarkably coffee-like, I could not help but be grateful for everything that had happened. I felt sadness for my home planet, but help was on the way and Nevak and I had already discussed our plan to stay on earth once they had liberated it. To Nevak's dismay, and my joy, he had been labeled too important to risk in combat, meaning that we would not be going to earth in the first wave. I was ok with this, as long as my race was liberated, I did not have to be there to see it, but I sure as hell wanted to get there once the fighting was over. Because, even though I enjoyed it here, I could never leave my home behind completely. I was glad that Nevak understood, and he supported my decision fully. My thoughts were interrupted by the sound of the sliding door opening.

"Hey, honey, I'm home," Nevak exclaimed as he walked in. I had taught him this archaic term in English and he had taken a shine to it. We had decided that it was important for us to learn each other's languages, so we no longer had to rely on technology to understand each other. The Zahothian language was fucking insane, so this was going to be a long process, but we were making strides each day. For now, we were still using the translator most of the time.

"Hi, honey," I answered and went up to him. Even with his child already in my belly, I could still not get enough of this man. I pulled his head down for a kiss the moment he walked in. He grabbed me by the hair and yanked back. God, I loved it when he got rough with me. He pushed me over the dining table and lifted up my Zahothian skirt and entered my eager pussy. Still pulling my head back he fucked me hard from behind until we both came hard. I loved feeling his cum erupt inside me. After he had used me for his pleasure he turned me around and got on his knees to kiss my stomach. I cradled his head in my hands and kissed his beautiful head.

It was the day of departure for the first Zahothian force and we were having a get-together of the people I had gotten to know so well over the past month. Chavak and Qroko were the guests of honor. Without either of them, none of this would have been possible. They were both shipping off to liberate earth in a matter of hours. All four of us stood together in our living area, Nevak's arm around me tightly.

"It has been an honor meeting you, Avi. I hope that our mission will be successful and man more of your kind will come to live with us on Zahoth," Qroko said warmly.

Chavak added, " Seeing you two makes me insanely jealous," Chavak added humorously, "I hope I find my own 'love' during our mission."

I touched Chavak's arm and told him that any human girl would be lucky to have him, and I really meant it.

Nevak gave both the warriors a strong hug and each of them kissed my stomach. I had gotten used to being the mother of the miracle child, so this was no longer weird to me. As Qroko hugged me goodbye, I whispered in his ear, "none of this would have happened without you."

He released his grip and nodded, I could have sworn I saw a tear come to his eye, but maybe I was imagining things. He was a massive warrior after all; I was not even sure he was capable of tears. I looked at the two warriors heading off to liberate my people and could not help but feel a deep love for both of them. Now, I just had to hope that they would succeed.

But in the meantime, I could not be happier with my man by my side and his baby in my belly. I was starting a new chapter in my life, one that I never thought would have been possible for a lowly miner. As the soldiers left, I hugged Nevak as tight as I could and thought about our future child.

SNEAK PEEK

Enjoy the first chapter of the next installment in the Guardians of the Universe series right now!

LIBERATED BY THE INVADER

Mya

"ASSES OUT OF BEDS! Roll call in 30!"

This was the opening to each day I had gotten so used to hearing. Before I rushed out of bed I scratched my 582nd notch into the rough, wooden wall against my bunk with a rusty nail I had hidden in my straw mattress. I could not complain too much though, I was one of the lucky ones. Out of the 54 people sleeping in my dorm (more of a barn really) I was one of 3 who was not yet sharing a bed. It was becoming clear that the stream of prisoners being hauled in every day had exceeded the camp's ability to house them. I did not want to be the one picked on today, so I got up with apparent eagerness and put on my clothes. These were the same clothes I had arrived in almost two years ago. Except for the coat which I had taken off of a friend of mine who died in a typhoid outbreak. Many of the diseases once eradicated had returned with a vengeance since this became the way of life for most people on the planet. Apparently, I had a pretty sharp immune system which, depending on perspective, could be seen as a positive or a negative. I join the line of dirty drones, myself included, slowly dragging themselves out into the freezing cold to receive their breakfast of boiled oats and daily bread ration. After this we have 30 minutes to get our gear together and line ourselves up for inspection.

It was not always like this. In my mind, I have gone through the events of the last 5 years trying to figure out what it was that got us into this predicament. And living here means I have had a lot of time to think about it. Everything seems to have gone downhill after the visit of the Zahothian ambassador and the subsequent disappearance of Avi 2564. Before this time, I was a reporter for the Global Gazette and living in Arkgan the largest city on the planet. I had a sense of purpose and security there and felt genuinely happy for a lot of my life. I believed in our supreme leader and the path he had put the planet on after the foundational war against the Zahothians. However, it turned out that this had all been a lie. I do not know exactly what happened to Avi 2564, but I know that since that day everything changed.

All 1300 of us stood out in the falling snow in a temperature that a polar bear would shiver in. Those who did not have coats were wrapped in dirty blankets they had scav-

enged from around the camp and those with broken shoes
had wrapped their feet tightly in rags, however, this would
not protect them from frostbite for long. I had decided
that if I was to ever lose any of my clothes I would just
walk in to the snow and never come back, rather than
freeze to death over the span of a month, or more. The
Nepharan guards counted every one of us and if there was
any discrepancy in the count, then we would be forced to
wait in the cold while it was sorted out. There was a time
when I had seen these aliens as the epitome of knowledge
and grace. I had the chance to meet one once about 6
years ago at a ball held in the supreme leader's honor.
Everyone in the room seemed captivated by the alien
dressed in his elegant robes and saying things of such
beauty and intelligence. It was not until later that the
manipulation techniques of the Nepharans became apparent. I am not sure anymore what actually happened at that
ball and whether he said any of these things or whether
they were simply projections in my brain of what I wanted
to hear. Anyway, those times were gone and now all of
humanity could see them for the monsters they truly were.
Their pale blue skin, long necks and beak-like noses now
filled me with a sense of fear, dread and disgust I did not
think I was capable of feeling.

Ever since the aliens murdered the supreme leader and all
of the highest officials of the planetary government, their
plans for earth had become more transparent. As we
marched along the now far too familiar desolate path
towards the mine shaft, I remembered that I had once
thought that some people were born to do this work, some

people were inherently inferior to me. I deserved to live in Arkgan and enjoy myself because I was a true believer in the global state, and those who did not, deserved to become slaves. Remembering this, I disgusted myself. How could have I been so damn blind? I even remember writing an article introducing Avi 2564 to the world and genuinely feeling that she did not deserve the honor of being earth's ambassador. Right, the honor of being fucked by a massive alien warlord, what a lucky girl. When Avi 2564 disappeared along with the Zahothian ship, we were fed a lie that the Zahothian ambassador had murdered her and that they intended to invade us once again. Without a body or any other sort of evidence this was the first piece of bullshit that actually stank to the people of earth in the last 100 years. It became apparent that we were being lied to and theories were circulating that it was , in fact, the Nepharans who had killed her. Riots broke out all over the globe, nowhere more than in the mining districts. Avi became a martyr for the cause and her picture was plastered everywhere. The security forces of the mines were overrun and all government personnel were hanged from the windows of the buildings. In Arkgan we were terrified by these uprisings and more than ever relied on our government to protect our privileged way of life, but this was not to be. Realizing that their lie had failed and that they were losing control of the human population, the Nepharans quickly took control of the planet themselves, no longer needing their human intermediaries and they were not playing around. They landed multiple forces on the planet and quickly squashed all rebellion in the most brutal fashion. All humans who disobeyed in anyway were immediately killed. They had absolutely no remorse and clearly taking human lives did not prick their conscience one bit. Th revolutionaries were slaughtered and no one dared to put up a fight once they had seen so many of their kind killed in such a brutal manner. It was of course necessary to replace all those that were killed and that's where the city folk, and yours truly, came in. We were all shipped off to different parts of the globe to work as slaves in their Barnox mines. There were no longer any lies about what we had been doing for the past 100 years. We had always been slaves, but now, we just knew that we were. Somehow, I preferred ignorance to the reality. Some people still hold out hope that the once dreaded Zahothians and Avi 2564 will rescue earth from its doom, but I think those people are deluded. It is clear to me that earth had been a pawn in the game of two races far superior to our own. It was like two children playing with an ant hill, they were not evil, they just did not care about the ants. I have resigned myself to the fact that I will live out the rest of my short life in this arctic hellhole and be remembered or loved by no one.

We reached the mine and put our pick axes to work. The question that has bothered me the most about all this is: why would an advanced alien race be using such primitive methods to get what they want? The only answer I can come up with is that this is basically free of cost. You do not have to pay slaves anything; you just have to keep them alive. At the beginning of my incarceration, this thought made me angry, but I did not feel anything anymore, even my hands or toes as I drew the axe above my head and brought it down almost in unison with the other thousand humans working the depths of this tundra. Every strike released a little more of this stuff to power the Nepharans' economy. At least, down in the mine I was out of the blizzard. When everything is taken from you, you will be happy about the smallest things. The Nepharans barely guarded us anymore, they seemed well-accustomed to wintry temperatures and just stood outside of the mine waiting for us to do our 10 hours of labor, before we would head back to the base and collapse on our bunks into a deep but restless sleep.

On our march back from the mine, I felt exhausted both physically and emotionally. The snow was falling harder and harder and I could barely make out the person in front of me. I was so deep in my thoughts that I did not know how much time had passed since I had strayed from the formation. I realized that I had wandered far from the path and was now completely lost. I could only see a few yards in front of me and had no way of getting back to the group in this weather. I plonked my butt down in the snow and shivering I came to accept that these might be my last hours on earth. The cold would probably kill me soon enough and, if not, then I would be executed by the Nepharan guards as a deserter. Death no longer scared me. I wept for my former life, but even that was based on a lie. I had reached a solemn acceptance of what was going to happen to me and closed my eyes and laid down in the snow to await my fate.

. . .

Suddenly, I saw a great flash of light and heard a deafening crash probably 50 feet to my right. I jumped up and rushed towards the sound. As I approached I saw pieces of a weird black and red substance scattered atop the formerly undisturbed white snow. I could see that the pieces were hot because they were melting everything around them. I continued on in my search and discovered the wreckage of a type of ship I had never seen before. It was badly beaten up, but I could tell that it was meant for space travel. I was startled by a commotion behind me, it sounded like the Nepharan guards had also taken an interest in this event. It was not long before they saw me standing at the edge of the crater, examining the alien object.

"What are you doing out of formation, human?" said the voice from within the blizzard. The snow had cleared up a little bit, but I could still only see an outline of my interrogator. I gave no answer just stood frozen in my spot. I heard a shot and fell on my stomach into the snow, paralysed with fear. Then, I heard the laugh of the guards as they approached me. In addition to the footsteps of the guards, I could hear a slight mechanical noise coming from the crater. It sounded like the ship was struggling to complete an action.

"Human scum. You will be executed for your desertion," one of the guards said as he pushed his bony foot, painfully, into the small of my back.

. . .

The rest of the guards stepped towards the crater to examine the wreckage. They were conversing in Nepharan as I suddenly heard three loud shots in quick succession. I turned my head in the snow and saw the three guards fall to the ground in a flood of black blood. I felt the foot holding me down disappear as the Nepharan let off a series of shots into the falling snow. He screamed something in Nepharan into the emptiness and suddenly I saw the shadow of a giant towering behind my captor. He sensed this and turned around swiftly, only to have his stomach impaled by a black, ridged sword. The blade went straight through his armour and out the other side of his back. The Nepharan gasped in shock and pain as the giant whispered something in his ear as he withdrew his weapon allowing the Nepharan to fall to the ground. His head bashed down into the snow and I could see the life leave his eyes merely feet from my position cowering in the snow. The giant red beast approached me and I could feel my heart attempting to burst out of my chest. I could now see him more clearly. He was dressed in a simple kilt-like garment which only covered his nether region. His body was covered in well-defined muscles, which became even more impressive with the deep red color his skin exhibited. He had a long pony-tail draped down over his strong tattooed chest from his otherwise bald head. His eyes were a deep black and I could make out a chiseled bone structure in his face as, to my surprise he knelt down next to me and gently tapped my shoulder. I looked straight at him, eyes wide open in nervous excitement. He took out a device from a sachet tied to his kilt that looked a little like a transparent pig's ear. Still in shock, I winced as he placed it on my ear and I felt a sharp twinge in my head as he pressed down on it. I was paralysed with fear and was certain he was going to kill me. But then the words that came out of his mouth stunned me:

"Hello, my name is Qroko."

ABOUT THE AUTHOR

Veronica Dean grew up reading science fiction, but as her tastes matured, she added some steamy romance into the mix. After a lifetime of reading the genre, she decided it she channeled some of that passion into her own stories. Veronica is obsessed with bold and dynamic heroines and the powerful dangerous aliens they cannot help but fall in love with.

When she is not typing away on her computer, you might find Veronica curled up on the couch with a glass of wine and book by one of her favorite authors; or maybe on a nature hike with her wonderful husband and their little sausage dog Winston.

Check out the Veronica Dean website to see her entire catalogue or sign up to her newsletter for some sizzling bonus material and to stay up-to-date with every new release.

Printed in Great Britain
by Amazon